First th̶e̶ ̶t̶e̶r̶r̶i̶b̶l̶e̶ accident that left cheerleader captain Jennifer paralyzed.

Then Bobbi Corcoran was scalded to death in the locker room shower.

Corky, Bobbi's sister, fought the evil and succeeded in burying it in the Fear Street cemetery . . . forever.

Or so she thought.

But the horrifying and fatal "accidents" have started again. What can Corky do, now that she knows . . .

THE EVIL IS BACK!

Books by R. L. Stine

Available from ARCHWAY Paperbacks

FEAR STREET
R·L·STINE

CHEERLEADERS
The Second Evil

AN ARCHWAY PAPERBACK
Published by POCKET BOOKS
New York   London   Toronto   Sydney   Tokyo   Singapore

AN ARCHWAY PAPERBACK *Original*

An Archway Paperback published by
POCKET BOOKS, a division of Simon & Schuster Inc.
1230 Avenue of the Americas, New York, NY 10020

ISBN: 0-671-75118-2

First Archway Paperback printing September 1992

15 14 13 12 11

Cover art by Edwin Herder

Printed in the U.S.A.

IL 7+

PART ONE

Where Is the Evil?

Chapter 1

Buried Hopes

Kimmy Bass slowed her car to a stop at Division Street and tapped her fingers impatiently on the wheel. "I never make this light," she complained.

Her friend Debra Kern stared out the passenger window at a boy in a blue windbreaker, walking a large Doberman across the street. "What's your hurry?" she asked, wiping steam off the window with her wool-gloved hand.

"You're always in such a hurry," Veronica (Ronnie) Mitchell chimed in from the backseat.

The light changed. Kimmy pushed hard on the gas pedal and the pale blue Camry lurched across the intersection. "I'm not in a hurry. I just don't like to stop," Kimmy said.

Debra shivered even though the heater was on high. She was very thin, and no matter how many T-shirts and sweaters she wore, she was always cold.

3

Ronnie looked completely lost inside the fake raccoon coat that had once belonged to her mother, but it kept her really warm. With her curly red hair, tiny snub of a nose, and freckles, she appeared to be about twelve.

Outside, the wind picked up, blowing dead brown leaves across the road. It was cold for late November. Heavy clouds hovered low in the evening sky, threatening snow.

"Want to do something Saturday night?" Kimmy asked, making a sharp turn onto Old Mill Road. "Hang out or something?"

Debra smoothed her straight blond hair with a quick toss of her head. Her blue eyes, normally pale and icy, lit up. "No. I actually have a date Saturday night."

"Hey, with who?" Ronnie asked, leaning over the front seat, catching the coy look on Debra's face.

"Eric Bishop," Debra said after a suspenseful pause.

Kimmy reacted with surprise. "Eric? Isn't he going with Cari Taylor?"

Debra's face assumed a smug grin. "Not anymore." She trailed her gloved finger along the steamed-up window, drawing a star across the glass.

Ronnie settled back in her seat. "Eric Bishop!" she exclaimed. "He's definitely okay." She snuggled inside the big, furry coat. "Could you turn the heat down a bit?"

Kimmy ignored her.

"Who are you interested in these days?" Debra asked Kimmy, adjusting her seat belt.

"I don't know," Kimmy replied wistfully. "Nobody, really."

4

"You're not still hung up on Chip, are you?" Debra asked, turning to study Kimmy's round face. In the light of the passing streetlights, she could see Kimmy's cheeks redden.

"No way!" Kimmy protested loudly. "Corky is welcome to him. Really."

Debra stared hard at her. Ronnie hummed to herself.

"Really!" Kimmy repeated. "I mean it. I'm over Chip. I'm glad he dumped me."

"Chip seems to like Corcorans," Debra said dryly, turning back to the houses passing outside the window. "First Bobbi, now her sister Corky."

The mention of Bobbi's name brought a chill to the car. Debra reached out to turn up the heat, but saw it was up all the way.

"Bobbi was so great looking," Ronnie said thoughtfully.

"She was the best cheerleader I ever saw," Debra added.

"I was so jealous of her," Kimmy admitted. "I still can't believe she's dead."

"Poor Corky," Debra said, lowering her voice nearly to a whisper. "She really looked up to her sister. I can't imagine what it would be like. I mean, if *my* sister died, I'd . . ." Her voice trailed off.

"Corky's been kind of weird lately," Kimmy said, keeping her eyes on the twin beams of white light ahead of her. "She barely talks to anyone."

"I was jealous of her and her sister too," Ronnie confessed. "I mean, they were so perfect with their perfect blond hair, and their perfect white teeth, and their perfect figures."

"I've tried being friendly with Corky," Kimmy said. "But she just keeps that sad expression on her face and isn't friendly at all. That's why I thought maybe the three of us could—"

"We've got to get Corky back on the cheerleader squad," Debra said, interrupting. "It was so strange when she quit last month. If she'd quit right when her sister died, I'd understand. But she waited a while to drop out."

"We'll get her back to normal," Ronnie said. "At least I hope she'll listen to us."

Kimmy made a right turn onto Fear Street. The sky immediately appeared to darken. Gusting winds swept around the small car.

"Too bad you're not in sixth period study hall. In the library," Debra said. "You should have seen Suki Thomas with Gary Brandt. Well, Suki was giving Gary a sex ed. class. They didn't even bother to go back to the stacks."

"She was kissing him?" Ronnie asked, leaning forward to hear Debra's soft, whispery voice.

"I guess you could call it that. I thought Mrs. Bartlett was going to have a cow."

All three girls laughed.

Their laughter was cut short as the car approached the Fear Street cemetery. Behind a weather-beaten rail fence, the weed-choked graveyard sloped up from the street. Eerie wisps of gray mist rose up between the crooked tombstones.

"Corky's family should move," Debra said, shuddering. "I mean, living so close to where Bobbi is buried. It's like a constant reminder."

"Corky visits Bobbi's grave all the time," Kimmy said, shaking her head.

"We've *got* to talk to her," Ronnie said heatedly. "We've got to make her forget about Bobbi and the evil spirit—"

"The evil spirit isn't dead," Debra said suddenly. "I can still feel it."

"Debra, stop," Kimmy said sharply.

"I know the evil spirit that killed Bobbi is still alive," Debra insisted quietly.

"Don't say that!" Ronnie cried.

"You've got to stop reading those stupid books," Kimmy said. "I can't believe you spend so much time with that stuff."

"I want to learn all I can about the occult," Debra replied. "Both of you should too. You were there that night. You were there in the cemetery and saw the evil spirit."

"I saw Corky fight it. And I saw it go back down into its grave," Kimmy replied impatiently, almost angrily. "Oh, I don't know *what* I saw. It was all a bad dream. I just want to forget about it. I don't want to read any of that occult mumbo jumbo, and I don't want to hear about it."

Debra fingered the crystal she had begun wearing around her neck soon after Bobbi's funeral. "But I can feel—" she started.

"I want to get on with my life!" Kimmy declared loudly. "I want—" She stopped in mid-sentence, her mouth open.

Ronnie and Debra followed Kimmy's gaze through the still-cloudy windshield. In the darkness of the cemetery they could see a solitary figure near the top of a small hill where the ground leveled out and some new graves stood.

Wisps of gray mist snaked along her feet. She had

7

one hand on the top of a gravestone, her head lowered as if talking to someone in the grave.

"It's Corky," Debra whispered. "What's she doing there?"

"I *told* you," Kimmy said, slowing the car to a a near-stop. "She visits Bobbi's grave all the time."

"But she'll *freeze!*" Debra declared with a shiver. "Honk the horn." She reached out to pound on the horn, but Kimmy pushed her hand away.

"No. Don't."

"Why?" Debra insisted.

"I think it's bad luck to honk at a cemetery."

"Now who's the superstitious one?" Debra scoffed. She peered out into the darkness.

"Does she see us?" Ronnie asked.

"No. She's still staring at the grave," Kimmy said. She rolled down her window. "I'll call to her."

She stuck her head out the window and called Corky's name. The gusting wind blew the name back into her face.

"She didn't hear you," Debra said, staring out at Corky's unmoving figure, frail and small surrounded by the rows of crooked gravestones.

Kimmy rolled up the window, her cheeks red, her expression troubled. She tossed back her black crimped hair and continued to watch Corky's dark figure among the gravestones.

"What do we do now?" Ronnie asked in a tiny voice.

Debra fingered her crystal as she stared out at Corky.

"I don't know," Kimmy replied. "I don't know."

* * *

Unaware that she was being watched, Corky Corcoran leaned against the cold granite of Bobbi's tombstone. Her face was wet with tears, silent tears that came without warning, without crying. Tears that spilled out like the words she spoke to her dead sister.

"I shouldn't come here all the time," Corky said, bending low, one arm resting on top of the stone. "I know I shouldn't. Sometimes I feel as if I'm pulled here. Almost against my will."

The wind howled through the bent trees that clung to the sloping hill. Corky didn't feel the cold.

"If only I could sleep," she said. "If only I could fall asleep and not dream. I have such frightening dreams, Bobbi. Such vivid, frightening dreams. Nightmares. Of that awful night here in the cemetery. The night I fought the evil spirit."

She sighed and wiped away the tears with her open hands. "I feel as if I'm still fighting the evil, Bobbi. I'm still fighting it even though I sent it down to its grave."

Corky pressed her hot face against the cool granite. "Bobbi, can you hear me?" she asked suddenly.

As if in reply, the ground began to shake.

"Bobbi?" Corky cried, pulling herself upright in surprise.

The entire hill trembled, the white gravestones quaking and tilting.

"Bobbi?"

A crack formed in the dirt. Another crack zigzagged across the ground like a dark streak of lightning.

As Corky gaped in disbelief, the ground over Bobbi's grave split open. The crack grew wider.

Wider.

A bony hand reached up to the surface.

9

Bits of flesh clung to the arm that followed the hand. Another hand clawed through to the surface. A heavy stench filled the air, invading Corky's nostrils.

The bony hands grappled at the edge of the crack, pulling, straining, until a head appeared, then two shoulders.

"It's *you!*" Corky cried in horror as her dead sister pulled herself up from the grave.

Chapter 2

Someone Is Watching

"Bobbi?"

Corky uttered the name in a choked whisper. Her breath caught in her throat.

As her dead sister rose up in front of her, Corky staggered back, bumping against Bobbi's gravestone, almost toppling backward over it.

"Bobbi, it's you!" she cried, dropping to her knees on the hard, frozen ground.

Her sister rose up, up, until she hovered over Corky. Then she glared down with sunken eyes. The skin on her face, green and peeling, sagged, ready to fall off. Her straight blond hair was caked with wet dirt and twigs.

"Ohh!" Corky uttered a low, horrified moan. Her entire body convulsed in a tremor of terror.

Her dead sister stared down at her as the winds swirled and the ground shook.

"What is it, Bobbi?" Corky managed to cry out. She stared up at the hideous, rotting figure of her sister, not wanting to see what had happened to her but unable to turn away.

"What is it, Bobbi? Why did you leave your grave? Do you want to tell me something?"

Corky was so horrified, so overcome by Bobbi's decaying form, she didn't know whether she had spoken the questions out loud or only thought them.

As she stared up at the sunken-eyed green face, Bobbi's mouth slowly began to open. The flaking, blackened lips parted as if about to speak. No sound emerged.

"Bobbi, what *is* it?" Corky demanded. "What do you want to tell me?"

The black lips opened wider.

The sunken eyes rolled back.

The winds swirled loudly.

Corky stared up expectantly, unable to get off her knees, gripped by horror.

The lips parted even wider, and a fat brown worm curled out from Bobbi's mouth.

"Nooooooo!"

Corky's shrill scream rose and swirled with the raging wind.

She covered her eyes and lowered her head, fighting the waves of nausea that rolled through her body.

When she looked back up a few seconds later, blinking hard, struggling to breathe, Bobbi was gone.

The ink black sky was clear. Pale moonlight filtered gently down.

The winds had stopped.

The cemetery was deserted. Silent.

The ground over her sister's grave wasn't split or cracked open.

It didn't happen, she realized.

It was another dream. Another nightmare about Bobbi.

I was asleep, Corky thought.

I was leaning against Bobbi's gravestone, and I fell asleep.

I'm always so tired these days. I never can fall asleep at night. I never sleep the night through because of the nightmares.

Yes. I was asleep.

She stared at the dark ground, solid, silent. I *must* have dreamed it, she thought. The ground trembling, the gravestones shaking and tilting. The bony hand reaching up through the crack in the earth. The grotesque figure of her sister, green and rotting, covered with dirt and insects.

All a hideous dream.

"What am I going to do?" she asked aloud. "What *can* I do to make these nightmares end?"

She turned back to the low gravestone, lowering her head to talk once again to Bobbi. "I'm not going to visit for a while," she said softly, her voice muted by the heavy chill in the air. "At least I'm going to try to stay away."

The wind picked up and gently stirred the trees. There seemed to be whispering all around.

"It's not that I want to forget you, Bobbi," Corky continued with a loud sob. "It's just that— It's just that I'm still alive, and I have to—"

She stopped abruptly. "I'm sorry. I'm not making any sense. I have to go. It's late, and I'm cold."

13

Bobbi is even colder, she thought. The grim thought made her shudder.

"Bobbi, I really—"

She stopped short and uttered a brief cry.

Something moved behind a tall marble monument. A squirrel?

No. It was too big to be a squirrel.

Staring into the darkness, surrounded by the ceaseless whispers, Corky saw a dark form hunkered down behind the monument. A hand moved, then was quickly pulled back. A head, the face hidden in shadow, poked out, then disappeared just as quickly.

Someone is here, Corky realized.

Someone is watching me.

The whispers grew louder as once again the wind swirled around her.

Before she realized it, she had pushed herself away from Bobbi's gravestone and was running down the sloping hill. Panting loudly, she made her way through the crooked rows of stones, her sneakers slipping on the wet grass, on the flat, dead brown leaves. Tall wet weeds swished against the legs of her jeans.

Without slowing, she glanced back.

And saw that he was following her.

It was a man, or maybe a boy. He had the dark hood of his sweatshirt pulled up over his head.

He was running fast, breathing hard, his breath steaming up over the dark hood.

She could see only a triangle of his face. Saw part of his nose and eyes. Hard, determined eyes. Angry eyes. Gray eyes, so pale they were almost colorless.

Pale gray ghostlike eyes.

Somebody—help me! Corky wanted to cry out, but she could only pant in terror as she fled.

His shoes pounded the ground. So close behind her. Or was that the pounding of her heart?

Who was he? Why was he spying on her? Why was he chasing her?

The questions made her dizzy as she ran, gasping in mouthfuls of the heavy, cold air. Ran through the darkness. Ran toward the street. Fear Street.

Her house was only a block away.

Would she make it?

She was nearly to the street.

Running hard. Her right side aching.

The footsteps pounding behind her.

"Ow!"

She cried out as her leg hit a low tombstone.

As the pain shot up her leg, she fell and toppled forward, her arms and legs sprawling out as she dropped facedown into a pile of wet leaves.

Chapter 3

"Please Come Back"

"Corky!"

At first she didn't recognize the voice.

"Corky!"

She raised her head, scrambled to her feet, frantically brushing at the wet leaves clinging to the front of her coat.

"Hey, Corky!"

The voice came from the street. From the little blue car just beyond the curb.

"Kimmy!" she cried. "Oh, Kimmy!"

Kimmy was running toward her, her eyes wide with concern. Behind Kimmy, Corky could see Debra and Ronnie climbing out of the car.

"He—he's chasing me!" Corky cried breathlessly She skidded to a stop.

Kimmy protectively threw her arms around Corky's shoulders. "What's wrong, Corky?"

17

"What *is* it?" Ronnie called, hurrying up to them.

"He's chasing me!" Corky turned and pointed behind her.

No one.

No hooded man. No pale, pale eyes.

Vanished.

Or was he another nightmare?

Corky shuddered. Her side ached. Her ankle throbbed from its collision with the granite tombstone.

Another nightmare? Just a hallucination?

"We've got to get you home," Kimmy said, her arm still around Corky's shoulders. "Come on, Corky. Come with us," she urged softly.

"It's freezing out here!" Ronnie exclaimed, wrapping her big coat tightly around herself.

Debra remained silent, staring up at the crooked gravestones in an old section of the cemetery. Intense concentration froze her face. She reached for the crystal she wore around her neck and, still gazing up at the old stones, moved her lips in some sort of silent chant.

"Debra, come *on!*" Kimmy's voice from near the car interrupted Debra's concentration. She turned, still distracted, and followed her friends to the car.

A short while later Kimmy pulled the Camry up the gravel drive beside the Corcorans' rambling old house and cut the engine.

The four girls jogged to the front porch. Corky fumbled with her keys before finally managing to push open the front door. They all stepped inside.

"Brrrrrr!" Debra shivered and stamped her feet.

"Debra, it isn't *that* cold," Kimmy scolded.

"Yaaaaii!"

A screaming figure leapt out at them from the living room.

"Sean, give us a break," Corky told her little brother, rolling her eyes.

"I scared you." Sean grinned, his blue eyes lighting up. With his straight blond hair and high cheekbones, he looked like a smaller, more angelic version of Corky.

"We don't really feel like being scared right now," Kimmy told him, tossing her coat onto the banister.

"Do you feel like playing Nintendo?" Sean asked, tugging her arm.

"Nintendo?"

"Yeah. I've got Mega Man II."

"Not right now," Kimmy told him.

"Just a short game," Sean insisted, pulling Kimmy toward the stairs.

Kimmy turned helplessly to Corky.

"Sean, take a hike," Corky said sharply. "We can't play with you now." She poked her head into the living room. "Where are Mom and Dad?"

Sean reluctantly let go of Kimmy's sleeve. "Next door."

"Come on in," Corky told the three girls, motioning to the living room. "I'm going to run into the kitchen and put on the kettle. I'll make hot chocolate."

"That sounds great!" Debra exclaimed, rubbing her shoulders, still shivering.

"I *hate* hot chocolate," Sean offered loudly.

"Sean, please!" Corky cried. She pointed. "Upstairs. Now."

"You're a jerk" was his reply, one he used about a

hundred times a day. He stuck his tongue out at her, then loped up the stairs to his room.

Corky clicked on the floor lamp beside the leather couch against the wall. Pale light washed over the living room, which was decorated mainly in greens and browns.

"I'll be right back," she told the others. She hesitated at the doorway. "What were you doing there? I mean, at the cemetery?"

Debra flashed Kimmy a hesitant look. "Well . . ."

"We were looking for you," Kimmy explained. "We were headed to your house. But we stopped when we saw you . . . uh . . ." She hesitated to finish her sentence.

Corky's pale cheeks reddened. "I was at Bobbi's grave. I go there sometimes."

No one could think of a reply. A heavy silence hung over the room.

"I'll go put on the kettle," Corky said and hurried out of the room.

As she held the kettle under the tap, her mind whirred from thought to thought. She tried to figure out why the three cheerleaders had come to find her.

Corky hadn't spent time with any of them since dropping off the cheerleading squad. They always acted very friendly when she passed them in the halls at school. But Corky really hadn't talked with them in weeks.

Hearing an odd noise, Corky glanced out the kitchen window into the darkness. Two cats were chasing each other over the deep carpet of brown leaves that covered the backyard. Their chase reminded her of being pursued by the strange hooded man with the cold gray eyes. With a shudder she hurried back to her visitors.

She found Kimmy and Debra seated on opposite ends of the couch. Kimmy was tapping her fingers nervously on the arm. Debra had her hands clasped tightly in her lap.

Ronnie was standing by the window, hands on her slender hips, staring out at the driveway. She turned when Corky reentered the room. "I think we're warming up," she said.

Corky moved quickly to the armchair that faced the couch. She sat down, and a rude noise erupted from under the chair cushion.

"Sean!" she screamed angrily, jumping to her feet. She reached under the cushion and pulled out her brother's pink whoopee cushion.

Her three visitors laughed.

"My family *loves* practical jokes," Corky explained, rolling her eyes. She tossed the flattened whoopee cushion across the room.

"Your brother's funny," Debra said, tucking her legs under her.

"You want him?" Corky offered. She resumed her place on the chair. Ronnie moved in front of the couch and flopped down on the carpet, crossing her legs in front of her.

"Corky, how *are* you?" Kimmy asked finally in a concerned tone.

"Okay, I guess," Corky replied quickly, avoiding Kimmy's eyes.

"Were you at the game last night?" Ronnie asked.

"No. Huh-uh." Corky shook her head.

An uncomfortable silence.

Corky cleared her throat. The repetitive electronic music of Sean's Nintendo game drifted down from upstairs.

"So why'd you want to see me?" Corky asked.

"We want you to come back on the squad," Ronnie blurted out.

"Yeah. That's why we came," Kimmy said, locking her blue eyes on Corky's.

"I don't know," Corky replied, shaking her head. She brushed away a strand of blond hair that had fallen over an eye.

"The squad really needs you," Kimmy said. "It isn't the same without you."

"Really," Ronnie added earnestly.

"That's nice of you," Corky said, avoiding their eyes. "But . . ."

Her mind suddenly returned to the days when Bobbi was on the squad. She remembered how angry Kimmy had been when Bobbi was named cheerleader captain. She remembered how Kimmy had tried to turn the other girls against Bobbi.

Now Kimmy was the captain. Bobbi was dead, and Kimmy had gotten what she always wanted. So why was she here begging Corky to rejoin the squad?

"Why not give it a chance?" Kimmy urged her.

"Yeah. Just come to practice a few times," Ronnie suggested, twirling an opal ring on her index finger.

"Let's be honest," Corky blurted out. "You girls all resented Bobbi and me."

Her blunt words seemed to freeze in the air. Kimmy and Ronnie looked stunned for a brief moment. Debra swallowed hard.

"Things have changed, Corky," Kimmy said finally. Then she added, "Since that night."

Debra dropped her hands to her lap. She stared out the window with her icy blue eyes, her face pale in the harsh light of the floor lamp.

"We've all changed, I think," Kimmy continued, lowering her voice. "I know I have."

Corky sighed but didn't say anything.

"I was there with you that night," Kimmy said heatedly. "I saw the evil spirit too. I saw the dirt flying up from that old grave. I—I can't get it out of my mind."

"I can't either," Ronnie added. "I still have nightmares about it."

"Me too," Debra whispered.

"It's changed me," Kimmy said, continuing to stare at Corky. "I didn't lose a sister like you did, but it's changed me. I used to be angry a lot of the time. You're right when you say I resented you and Bobbi. I'm not as thin or as pretty or as talented as you. But after that horrible night in the cemetery, I don't care so much about that stuff. I saw how fragile life is. I saw—"

"It made us all stop and think about what's important," Ronnie interrupted. "I've changed too."

"And you've changed too," Kimmy told Corky. "We've all seen it. We understand."

Debra nodded but remained silent.

"That's why we think it would be good for you to come back to the squad," Ronnie said. "We really want to help."

"We should be friends," Kimmy said, round spots of pink growing darker on her cheeks. "We went through something really frightening together. Now we should be friends."

Corky stared at them one after another.

They're sincere, she decided. They really mean it. They came here out of friendship, out of concern for me.

They really have changed.

Corky had a sudden urge to leap across the coffee table and hug all three of them. Instead, she stammered, "It—it's really nice of you. To come, I mean. I mean, to ask me back. I'll think about it. I really will."

"Come to practice after school," Kimmy urged. "You can just watch, if you want."

"Well . . ." Corky climbed to her feet and, wrapping her arms over the front of her sweater, crossed over to the window.

"The spark is just missing without you," Ronnie said, her eyes following Corky across the room.

"We haven't replaced you," Kimmy added. "Your place on the squad is waiting for you. Really."

"Thanks," Corky said, sincerely moved.

She gazed out the window—and gasped. "Ohh! It's *him!*"

The hooded man with the strange, ghostly eyes—he must have followed her home.

As Corky gaped in fright, he strode over the shadowy front lawn, moving quickly toward the house.

Chapter 4

The Evil Is Alive

"Corky, what *is* it?"

Seeing the horrified expression on Corky's face as she stood frozen at the window, Kimmy and Debra leapt off the couch and darted across the room. Ronnie, who had scrambled to her feet, was right behind them.

"He—he's there!" Corky managed to cry. She pointed toward the middle of the yard.

Kimmy put a protective arm around Corky's shoulders and drew her aside.

The other two girls pressed their faces close to the glass and peered out.

"Huh?"

"Where?"

"He's there!" Corky insisted, her voice trembling. "He stared at me with those empty eyes. Like ghost eyes."

"I don't see him," Debra said, cupping her hands around her eyes to shut out the glare from the living room.

"I don't see *anything,*" Ronnie agreed. "The wind is blowing the leaves around. That's all."

"Hey, there are two cats down at the end of the drive," Debra reported. She turned away from the window to face Corky. "Is *that* what you saw?"

"No!" Corky insisted, shaking her head. "I *saw* him. I *did!* He was there, walking on the grass toward the house."

"Well, he's gone now," Ronnie said, flashing Kimmy a puzzled look.

Corky breathed a loud sigh of relief. "He must have seen us all staring at him and run away," she said.

"Yeah. I guess," Debra said doubtfully.

"I guess," Ronnie repeated.

They don't believe me, Corky thought miserably. They don't believe I saw him.

They think I'm seeing things.

And then she added, *I'm* not so sure I believe me.

She shuddered and started back to the couch.

"Guess we'd better get going," Kimmy said, starting toward the front hallway. "I promised my parents I'd be back half an hour ago."

"Me too," Ronnie said, forcing a smile for Corky.

"It was really nice of you to come," Corky said, a little embarrassed at how stiff the words sounded. "I mean, I'm so glad you came by. With that guy and everything—"

Again Ronnie met Kimmy's eyes.

None of them believe me, Corky thought again, catching Ronnie's expression. They think I'm cracking up.

26

She glanced at the front window, half expecting to see the hooded guy peering in at her.

The window was dark and empty.

Kimmy and Ronnie had pulled on their coats.

"Is that fake fur? It's really neat!" Corky ran her hand up and down the sleeve of Ronnie's coat.

"You like it? There's room for you in here too," Ronnie joked.

"Hey, aren't you coming?" Kimmy called to Debra, who had hung back at the living-room doorway.

"I thought I'd stay a few minutes and talk with Corky," Debra told Kimmy. She turned to Corky. "If that's okay?"

"Yeah. Sure," Corky replied quickly, smiling at Debra.

"I'll walk home," Debra told Kimmy.

"I can drive you," Corky said.

"Well, think about what we said," Kimmy told Corky, pulling open the front door. "Come to practice, okay?"

"I'll think about it. I really will," Corky replied.

More good-nights. Then Kimmy and Ronnie disappeared out the door.

Corky followed Debra back into the living room. They both headed for the couch. The beams of Kimmy's headlights rolled up the wall, then disappeared.

Debra tucked her legs under her slight frame and settled onto the cushion. "How *are* you, Corky? I've been meaning to come over for a long time."

"I'm okay, I guess," Corky said, sitting on the arm of the couch at the far end from Debra.

"No. I mean *really*," Debra said, her blue eyes suddenly glowing with intensity, burning into Corky's. "I mean, how are you *really*?"

"Not great," Corky admitted. "I mean, it's been hard. Real hard. You were there that night, Debra. It must be hard for you too."

Debra nodded solemnly. "Kimmy and Ronnie think I've gone weird." Her hand went up to the crystal at her neck. "They think I'm weird because I've become so interested in the occult. But I can't get over what happened."

Corky uttered a dry laugh. "We've all gone a bit weird, I think."

Debra didn't smile. "They told me not to tell you this, but I have to. They made me swear I wouldn't say it, but I don't care. I have to let you know, Corky."

Corky walked to the window, turned, and rested her back against the sill. "Let me know what? Why are you being so mysterious, Debra?"

"The evil is still here," Debra said flatly, her eyes suddenly dull as if someone had turned off a light inside her.

Corky's mouth dropped open, but no words came out.

Debra shifted uncomfortably on the couch.

The awful jangling music from the Nintendo game upstairs seemed to grow louder.

"You were there, Debra," Corky said, her voice nearly a whisper. "You saw me fight poor Jennifer. You saw the evil spirit pour out of her mouth. You saw the evil go down into Sarah Fear's coffin where it was buried again. You saw it all, Debra."

Debra nodded, keeping her lifeless eyes locked on Corky's. "I saw. But I know the evil didn't die, Corky. You didn't kill it. Believe me. It's still around."

"But, Debra, maybe . . ."

Corky wasn't sure *what* to say. Kimmy and Ronnie were right—Debra had gotten strange. She had always been a little quiet, a little cold even. But sitting there so straight on the couch, her legs tucked under her, dressed all in black, her pale face frozen in that stare, Debra looked positively frightening.

"Kimmy and Ronnie don't believe me," Debra said, clasping her hands in front of her almost as if preparing to pray. "But I'm right, Corky. The evil spirit is still around. I can feel the evil. I can feel it so strongly—right now—right in this house!"

"Please stop!" Corky cried. She pushed herself away from the window and walked back to the couch, stopping a few inches in front of Debra. "These books you've been reading. About voodoo and the occult—"

"I've been studying," Debra replied, sounding defensive. "I know what I'm talking about, Corky." She suddenly reached up and grabbed Corky's hand. "We were never friends. I know I was never nice to you, or to your sister. But we have to be friends now. We *have* to trust each other."

Debra's hand was burning hot.

Corky pulled away.

Debra let her hand fall back in her lap.

Corky sat down beside her on the couch. "We have to forget what happened," Corky heard herself say.

Debra shook her head, frowning. "We can't. Not while the evil is still here."

"Maybe you should stop reading all that stuff,"

Corky said softly. "We've all been through a terrible experience. But we have to get on with our lives now. We have to force ourselves. I know that's why Kimmy and Ronnie asked me back on the squad."

"You're not *listening* to me," Debra insisted. "The evil spirit is alive. You didn't kill it, Corky. There's no way we can get on with our lives—not while it's still here. You've got to believe me!"

"Debra, your hand is so hot. Do you have a temperature?" Corky asked.

A shrill whistle interrupted their conversation.

"Oh, no! I forgot all about the hot chocolate!" Corky hurried toward the kitchen.

"Let it whistle. I've been reading about ancient spirits," Debra said. "I—"

"Sit still. We need something hot to drink," Corky interrupted. "I'll be right back."

She hurried out of the room, her mind spinning, Debra's words echoing in her ears.

Poor Debra, Corky thought. She seems as troubled as I am. She looks so pale, so tense, so . . . frail.

What can I say to her? she asked herself after turning off the teakettle. What does she *expect* me to say?

I don't believe the evil spirit is still alive. I saw it buried.

I saw it. We all saw it.

But what if it's true? What if it isn't buried?

What then?

Is Debra trying to scare me? Corky suddenly wondered. Is she saying all this just to keep me from going back on the squad?

No. Debra believed what she was saying. It was

30

obvious from the expression on her face, from the dull horror in her eyes.

Corky pulled two mugs down from the cabinet and glanced out the kitchen window.

Was that a figure she saw in the backyard? Was someone out there?

She looked again and saw nothing. It must be my imagination, Corky reasoned. She poured the chocolate powder into each mug, all the while peering nervously out the window into the dark yard.

"Hey, Corky?" Debra called from the living room.

"Be right there!" Corky shouted back to her. "I'm just going to pour the hot water."

She lifted the kettle off the stove and carried it to the mugs on the counter.

As she reached the counter, her arm suddenly flew straight up.

Without wanting to, she raised the steaming kettle over her left hand.

"Hey!" she cried out.

She tried to lower her right arm, struggling to push the kettle back down.

To lower it.

To move it away from her left hand.

But her arm wouldn't obey her.

She had no control over it.

And her left hand wouldn't move away from the countertop.

"What's happening? What's *happening* to me?"

Holding the kettle high, her right hand tilted the kettle down.

Down.

Down.

31

Steam rose from the spout. Then the scalding water began to shower down on her left hand.

"Help! Ow!"

She couldn't lower her arm, couldn't move her hand out from under the boiling waterfall.

"Help me—please!" she cried.

The scalding water gushed over the back of her hand, splashing up her arm.

"I can't stop! Can't stop!"

The scalding water splashed onto her skin.

Burning.

Burning.

Burning beyond pain.

Beyond all sensation.

Chapter 5

Out of the Grave

"She's up in her room," Sean told Chip.

Chip tossed his Shadyside High letter jacket onto the banister and pulled down the sleeves of his bulky sweater. "Is it okay to go up?" he asked.

Sean blew a large pink bubble before replying. "Yeah. Kimmy's up there too."

Chip frowned. He glanced up to the top of the stairs. He didn't really want to see Kimmy. It had been two months since he'd broken up with her and gone out with Bobbi Corcoran. But Kimmy still treated him coldly and made him feel uncomfortable every time they bumped into each other. When they passed in the halls at school, she always turned away, cutting him dead.

"Is Corky feeling okay?" Chip asked Sean, delaying the confrontation.

Sean nodded, unsticking bubble gum from his cheeks. "Yeah, she's okay. Only she can't wrestle."

"That's too bad," Chip replied, chuckling. He was trying to decide whether to go upstairs or not. "Maybe I'll come back later," he told Sean.

"Chip, is that you?" Corky's voice called from upstairs.

Trapped, he thought.

"Hi!" he shouted and stepped past Sean to climb the stairs.

He stopped in the doorway to Corky's bedroom. She was sitting on the edge of the bed, her bandaged hand resting in her lap. Kimmy was standing by the dresser, zipping up her down coat.

"How you doing?" Chip asked Corky, flashing her a broad smile.

"A lot better," Corky said, smiling back.

Chip crossed the room and bent down to give her a quick kiss on the cheek. After Bobbi's death, he and Corky had become friends. Corky found that he was someone she could talk to, about her sister, about her feelings of grief, about her fears. After a while they had become more than friends.

A tall, athletic-looking boy with an open, friendly face, Chip was wearing a heavy wool plaid sweater, all greens and blues, which made him look big and broad shouldered. His thick brown hair was unbrushed as usual.

"So the hand is better?" he asked Corky.

"Don't mind me. I'm just leaving," Kimmy interrupted, her voice dripping with bitterness.

"Oh, hi, Kimmy," Chip said, trying to sound casual. He didn't turn to her. He didn't want to see the disapproval on her face.

34

"Thanks for coming," Corky told Kimmy, standing up. "And thanks for bringing my homework."

"See you Monday," Kimmy said. With a toss of her black crimped hair, she strode quickly from the room.

As soon as she was gone, Chip stepped forward and wrapped his arms around Corky's shoulders, drawing her into a hug.

"Ow. Be careful. My hand!" she exclaimed.

"Hey, what are you two doing?" a voice shouted from the bedroom doorway.

They both looked around to see Sean, hands on hips, staring suspiciously at them.

"We're not *doing* anything," Corky said defensively.

Sean glared at her. "I thought you said you couldn't wrestle. You were wrestling with *him.*" He pointed accusingly at Chip.

"We weren't wrestling," Corky said, laughing. "Now get lost."

"Make me." Sean's standard reply.

"Go on. Beat it," Corky insisted.

Sean put his tongue between his lips and made a rude sound. Another of his standard replies.

Chip laughed.

Corky elbowed Chip in the ribs. "Don't encourage him," she chided. She glared at her brother. "Go on. Get lost."

"Okay," he said, pouting. "I'm going." Sean started out of the room, but turned at the doorway. "But no wrestling, you hear?"

He disappeared, and Corky heard him clomping back down the stairs.

"He's funny," Chip said, still chuckling.

35

"Who needs funny?" Corky asked dryly. She dropped back onto the edge of the bed.

Chip sat down beside her. "So the hand—it's really better?"

"Yeah. It's still pretty tender. You have no idea how hard it is to dress yourself with one hand!" She laughed, a forced laugh. "I'm going back to school on Monday," she told him. "It's been a long week. A long week."

He started to say something, but the phone on the night table rang. Corky sprang up to answer it.

"Oh. Hi. Yeah. Can I call you back later?" she said, holding the receiver in her right hand. "Chip just arrived. Okay. Bye."

She hung up the phone and, catching a glimpse of herself in the dresser mirror, ran her uninjured hand through her blond hair, smoothing it back.

"Who was that?" Chip asked, lying back on the quilted bedspread, resting his head on his hands.

"Debra," she replied. "She calls me every afternoon now. Ever since I burned my hand and she ran next door to get my parents, I think she feels responsible for me or something."

"Is she still insisting that the evil spirit made you burn yourself?" Chip asked, frowning.

Corky crossed to the window and looked down on the backyard. The late-afternoon sun had lowered itself behind the trees, making shadows stretch all across the leaf-covered lawn.

"Don't make fun of Debra," she said in a low voice.

"Hey, I'm sorry," Chip replied quickly. "It's just that she's gone weird or something. People accidentally burn themselves all the time, Corky. Your right hand slipped. The water poured onto your left hand. And—"

"My hand didn't slip," Corky said shrilly. "It wasn't an accident, Chip." She decided she had to tell him what really happened.

Chip pulled himself up to a sitting position. His face revealed his surprise. "You mean you *believe* her?" he asked, his voice rising several octaves.

"I don't have to believe *her*," Corky replied sharply, staring at him now. "I was there. I *know* what happened. I could feel the evil, Chip, I could feel it paralyze me. The evil spirit was there. It forced me to scald myself. It held my hand there and *forced* me!"

"Okay. Okay. Sorry," Chip muttered. He didn't like to fight with her. He almost always backed down or changed the subject. "That scary guy hasn't shown up again?" he asked. "The one with the gray eyes?"

"No sign of him," Corky replied. She shook her head bitterly. "Kimmy and Ronnie are sure that I made him up. Every time I started to point him out, he'd vanish. Poof." She snapped her fingers.

"Weird," Chip replied. He couldn't think of anything else to say. "So do you—"

"I never told you, I talked to a psychiatrist," Corky interrupted, walking back to the bed and sitting down next to him.

"Huh?"

"At the hospital," she told him, "when I told the emergency-room doctors how I burned my hand, they called for a psychiatrist to see me. I guess they thought I did it deliberately or something." She rolled her eyes.

Then Corky's expression grew thoughtful. As she

talked, she smoothed the bedspread with her unbandaged hand.

"He was a young guy. Really nice. His name was Dr. Sterne. He was the psychiatrist Mayra Barnes saw for a while."

Chip reacted with surprise. "Mayra? What did *she* need him for? She's got to be the most normal person in Shadyside!"

"She told me she started sleepwalking suddenly a couple of summers ago," Corky told him. "This Dr. Sterne helped her a lot."

"So what did he say to you?" Chip asked. "Did you tell *him* about the evil spirit?"

Corky turned her eyes to the window, avoiding Chip's stare. "Well, actually . . . no."

"Huh?"

"I just didn't want to get into it with him," she confessed. "I mean, I wasn't ready. I didn't want him to think I was totally crazy. I told him about Bobbi dying and everything—"

"And what did he say?" Chip demanded.

"He said I should try to return to a normal routine. He said I've been through a lot. But I have to stop dwelling on the past. I have to try to get my life back on track." She grabbed Chip's hand and squeezed it. "He was very understanding."

"What's a normal routine?" Chip asked. "You mean like early to bed, early to rise, or something?"

"Don't be dumb. He means I should try to do things the way I did before—before Bobbi died and that evil spirit . . ." Her voice trailed off. "I mean, I'm thinking of going back on the cheerleading squad."

"Outstanding!" Chip exclaimed with genuine enthusiasm.

"Well, I thought I'd give it a try," Corky said, still resting her hand on his. "Kimmy and Ronnie have been insisting, so . . ."

"Excellent," Chip said, squeezing her hand. "Excellent."

"I'm going to rejoin for two reasons," Corky said, her voice a whisper, her expression thoughtful. "I know I have to adjust to not having Bobbi around anymore. Getting back on the squad will keep me busy. You know, give me something to think about."

"And what's the second reason?" Chip asked.

"I have to find the evil spirit," she said, locking her eyes on his. "The evil is back. It must be inhabiting someone else. Maybe someone I know."

"Huh? What makes you so sure?" Chip demanded.

"Because it was right in my house the other night," Corky said in a whisper, staring down at the floor. "I'm going to find it before it kills again."

Chip stared at her thoughtfully, but didn't reply.

She raised her eyes to his. "I have one favor to ask. Sort of a big one," she said reluctantly.

"Yeah?" Chip eyed her warily. "What is it?"

"Come with me to the cemetery tonight after dinner?" She asked in a tiny, pleading voice.

"Huh?" He swept his hand back through his thick, disheveled hair.

"Come with me. I want to go to Bobbi's grave. Just one more time. I promised myself I'd stop going there so often. But I just want to tell Bobbi my decision. About going back on the cheerleading squad."

Chip sighed. "Bad idea," he said softly.

Corky squeezed his hand. "Come on, Chip."

"It's a bad idea, Corky," he repeated heatedly. "You said that shrink wants you to get back to a normal

39

routine. Well, going to the cemetery all the time isn't normal. I don't think you should go."

She leaned over and pressed her cheek against his. "Come on," she pleaded softly. "One last time. I promise."

She kept her face pressed against his. He turned toward her. She kissed him tenderly. A long kiss. A pleading kiss.

When she finally pulled her face away from his, she could see his features soften.

"Okay, okay. I'll go with you after dinner." And then he added, "I guess there's no harm. What could happen?"

It was a warm night for early December. Thousands of tiny white stars dotted the charcoal sky. A huge full moon cast bright light over the Fear Street cemetery.

Since the cemetery was little more than a block from Corky's house, she and Chip walked. He carried a flashlight, in case the moonlight wasn't enough, swinging it as they walked.

She asked him about last Saturday's basketball game, the first preseason one. He told her about the center on the opposing team who repeatedly slam-dunked even though he was the smallest guy on the floor! She told Chip how Sean had slipped green food coloring into the mashed potatoes just before dinner.

Neither of them talked about what they were doing, where they were headed. It was as if they were pretending they were out for a pleasant walk, and not going to the Fear Street cemetery so Corky could talk to the dead sister she couldn't get out of her thoughts.

After leaving the sidewalk, they made their way

through an old section of the cemetery, past rows of low, crumbling gravestones, jagged shadowy forms in the gray moonlight. Chip's flashlight sent a cone of bright light over the tall grass ahead of them.

Corky stopped and grabbed Chip's arm as two eyes appeared in that light. A scrawny white cat stepped timidly out from behind a granite gravestone. It mewed a warning, then scampered away, disappearing into the darkness.

Corky held on to Chip's arm and led him up a hill toward a section of newer graves on a flat grassy area bounded by low trees. "This way. We're almost there," she whispered.

Chip suddenly held back.

She stopped and followed the direction of his gaze. He was shining the light on a grave marker, its smooth whiteness revealing that it was new.

Jennifer Daly's grave.

Corky sighed and tugged the sleeve of Chip's sweater. Every time she passed that grave, terrifying memories flooded her mind. She didn't want that to happen now. She didn't want to think of poor Jennifer or the evil spirit that had inhabited her body.

She wanted to tell Bobbi her decision and then leave the cemetery. Leave the horror behind. Leave the memories behind.

Or at least try to.

Hearing a sound on the street, she turned around. Just a passing station wagon.

When she looked back down toward the old section, her eye caught a tilted hundred-year-old tombstone lit up by the bright moon. Corky knew it well. Surrounded by four other graves, Sarah Fear's stone, worn by time and the weather, stood silent.

It was over Sarah Fear's grave that Corky had battled the evil spirit on that dreadful, terrifying night. Over Sarah Fear's open grave, she had fought and won—and sent the evil pouring out of Jennifer Daly's body, back into the grave forever.

Or so she had thought.

But the evil hadn't remained in the grave.

The evil was back.

Somewhere.

Corky shuddered.

I don't want to think about this now.

I don't. I don't. I don't.

"This way," Corky said, turning away and striding with renewed purpose up to her sister's rectangular grave marker. Remnants of the flowers Corky had brought there a week ago lay shriveled at the foot of the stone.

Suddenly chilled, Corky shoved her hands deep into the pockets of her windbreaker and turned back to Chip. He was leaning against a tree several yards away, his arms crossed over his chest, his eyes on the sky.

I guess he's giving me a little space, Corky thought.

She turned to face her sister's gravestone. "It's me, Bobbi," she said in a low voice. "I'm really not going to be coming here for a while. At least I'm going to try not to come. I need to get my life back to normal. I know you'd want me to."

Corky paused, glanced at Chip who was still staring at the heavens, took a deep breath, and continued. "I just wanted to tell you about the decision I've made. I hope it's the right one. I've decided to go back on the cheerleading squad. You see, Bobbi—"

Corky stopped. She heard a sound. She turned and peered down the hill.

Her breath caught in her throat.

She froze.

And stared in horror as a woman floated out of Sarah Fear's grave.

Chapter 6

Five Mysterious Deaths

As the woman materialized in the shadows, Corky struggled to find her voice. Finally she managed to call out Chip's name.

Uncrossing his arms, he turned to her, startled. Corky pointed.

Would Chip see the woman too? Or was she seeing things again?

Corky was suddenly filled with dread. Was she losing her mind completely? Had she really seen this woman float up from Sarah Fear's grave?

"Hey!" Chip shouted. He saw the woman too.

Corky realized she'd been holding her breath. She let it out with a loud *whoosh*.

"Oh. Hi!" the woman called up to them.

The beam from Chip's flashlight played across her face as he made his way down toward her. She was young and kind of plain, Corky saw. She had straight black hair that hung down over the turned-up collar of her trench coat.

She raised her hands to shield her eyes from the light. "You scared me," she called out. "I didn't know anyone else was here."

Chip lowered the light to the ground and stood waiting for Corky to catch up. Reluctantly she followed.

"You scared us too," Chip said as he and Corky joined the young woman.

"I thought you were a ghost or something," Corky said, trying to make it sound light.

The young woman didn't smile. "I'm just doing a gravestone rubbing," she said. She had a scratchy voice, a voice that sounded older than she looked. "Did you two come here to be alone?"

Without waiting for an answer, she knelt in front of Sarah Fear's gravestone, then lay down on her stomach to work.

"Oh!" Corky couldn't help but utter a cry. The young woman was lying in the exact same place over the grave where Jennifer Daly had died.

Stop! Stop! Stop! Corky cried silently to herself. Stop thinking about it!

But how could she not be reminded when this woman was lying in the exact place?

"What are you doing?" she asked, speaking loudly to try to force away the horrible memories.

"I just told you—I'm doing some gravestone rubbings," the woman answered, rapidly moving a piece of black chalk over a thin sheet of paper she had taped over the tombstone. "There are some wonderful stones in this graveyard. Some of them are truly unique. Many are very revealing of their time, I think."

She finished quickly, then climbed to her feet, examining her work. Seemingly pleased, she rolled up the paper and smiled at Corky. "I'm kind of glad not to be alone," she said pleasantly. "This cemetery has an *amazing* reputation."

"I know," Corky said dryly.

"How can you work in the dark?" Chip asked, pointing to the rolled-up paper in her hand.

"I do most of it by feel, and I have a flashlight and, of course, the moon."

Chip wanted to ask more but didn't.

"I'm a graduate student doing research on Shadyside history." She stuck out her hand to Chip. "I'm Sarah Beth Plummer."

Chip and Corky shook hands with her and introduced themselves.

She seems quite pleasant, Corky thought, once you get used to the old-lady voice with her young face. Corky guessed that Sarah Beth was in her early twenties.

"Do you know anything about Sarah Fear?" Corky asked, staring at the gravestone in front of them.

The question seemed to surprise Sarah Beth; she narrowed her dark eyes and shook her head. "Not very much. I've read a little about her. In old newspapers, mostly. I know she came to a strange and mysterious end."

"Huh? Really?" Corky asked with genuine interest, her voice rising several octaves. "What happened to her?"

Sarah Beth pulled the collar of her trench coat tight. She shivered. "It's getting really cool, don't you think?" she asked, glancing toward the street. Then she added, "Are you really interested in Sarah Fear?"

"Yeah," Corky replied quickly. "It's . . . it's a long story, but I'm very interested." She cast Chip a look, urging him to respond.

"Uh . . . me too," Chip said obediently, placing a hand protectively on Corky's shoulder.

"Well, there's a small coffee shop on Hawthorne," Sarah Beth said, buttoning the top button on the coat. "It's within walking distance. It's called Alma's. It's sort of a college hangout."

"I know where it is," Chip said. "It's just a couple of blocks from here."

"If you want," Sarah Beth continued, "we could go there and get something hot to drink. I'll tell you all I know about Sarah Fear."

"Excellent," Chip said, glancing at Corky.

"Okay," Corky agreed.

The image of Sarah Beth floating up from Sarah Fear's grave flashed into Corky's mind again. She hesitated.

I imagined it, she told herself. *Just as I imagined Bobbi rising up from the ground.*

Sarah Beth seems friendly and interesting.

Taking one last glance up toward Bobbi's headstone, she turned and followed Chip and Sarah Beth to the street.

It took only a few minutes to walk to the restaurant at the corner of Hawthorne and Old Mill Road. "See that place over there?" Sarah Beth asked, pointing to a small redbrick house across the street. "That's where I'm living. It's not a mansion, but it's cozy."

Alma's coffee shop was small but cozy too. A long

counter ran along the right wall. Narrow red vinyl booths lined the other wall. The restaurant smelled of strong coffee and grilled onions.

Four teenagers at a booth near the front were laughing loudly, drumming on the tabletop and clattering their silverware. Two white-haired men nursing mugs of coffee at the counter were the only other customers.

Sarah Beth squeezed into the last booth at the back. Corky and Chip slid in across from her. Sarah Beth ordered tea, while Corky asked for hot chocolate. Chip ordered a Coke float with chocolate ice cream. "I have a craving," he said, shrugging his broad shoulders in reply to the stares of the other two.

The conversation was awkward at first. Corky began to wonder why she had agreed to come with this complete stranger. Sarah Beth seemed friendly enough. But Corky had an uneasy feeling about her, a suspicion she couldn't put into words.

"Why do you have to do your gravestone rubbing at night?" she asked Sarah Beth.

Again Sarah Beth's eyes narrowed, as if the question displeased her. "Oh, I'm just running late, as usual," she said, stirring her tea. "The assignment is due tomorrow morning, so of course I waited till the last possible minute."

It seemed like a perfectly reasonable explanation. But to Corky's mind, it just didn't ring true.

"Oops! Sorry." Chip dropped his ice-cream spoon onto the seat. Moving to retrieve it, he accidentally bumped Corky's hand.

She cried out in pain, startling Sarah Beth.

"It's my hand. I . . . uh . . . burned it," Corky explained, holding up her bandaged hand.

49

Sarah Beth continued to stare at her. For a frightening moment Corky had the feeling that Sarah Beth knew *how* she had burned it.

But of course that was impossible.

Stop being so suspicious, Corky scolded herself.

"Please tell us about Sarah Fear," she urged Sarah Beth. "I'm really interested."

Sarah Beth took a long sip of tea, then set the mug down. She reached for the aluminum sugar dispenser. "Okay, here's the little information I've been able to find," she said, pouring a stream of sugar into the tea.

"There isn't much information available about her. Strangely enough, I've been able to find out a lot more about her *death* than about her life.

"She married a grandson of Simon Fear, a mysterious man who moved to Shadyside and built an enormous mansion back in the woods, away from everyone else in—"

"That's the burned-out old shell across from the cemetery," Chip interrupted, busily scooping ice cream out of the tall soda glass.

"There wasn't much of a cemetery when Simon built his house," Sarah Beth replied. "He was all alone out here for a while. Then they built the mill in this area. Soon after that, the city built a road through the woods, right past the Fear mansion. And it came to be named Fear Street."

"Wow, I never knew any of this," Corky said, intrigued. "Of course my family is new in town. We just moved here this fall from Missouri. Have you lived in Shadyside a long time? Is that why you're so interested in the town?"

Sarah Beth took a sip of her tea, staring over the

booths to the front window of the restaurant. "I've lived here on and off," she replied curtly.

Am I being too nosy? Corky wondered. Is that why she got so cold?

"As I said, Sarah Fear married Simon's grandson. She and her husband lived in a house near Simon's mansion, a large house on Fear Lake."

"That's the small lake with the island in the middle of it," Chip explained to Corky. "It's back in the woods, two or three blocks from your house."

"As I mentioned earlier, little is known of Sarah Fear's life," Sarah Beth continued, rolling the sugar dispenser between her long, slender hands. "Her husband died suddenly of pneumonia just two years after they were married, leaving her quite wealthy, according to the newspaper reports from the time. She had servants. Her house was always filled with people. After her husband died, her two brothers moved in with her, as did several cousins.

"Despite her wealth, she was never mentioned on the social pages of the newspaper. Nor was she ever mentioned as being involved with charitable functions, the way wealthy people often are.

"I haven't found much personal information about her," Sarah Beth continued. "I don't know if she ever remarried. There isn't any mention of it in the Fear family records I've seen. Of course, she didn't live long enough to have much of a life."

"She died young too?" Corky asked in surprise.

"Very," Sarah Beth replied somberly. "In her twenties. Sarah died in 1899. The whole thing was very mysterious. The Fear family pleasure boat capsized on Fear Lake—for no apparent reason. It was a calm,

51

sunny summer day. The lake was as flat as glass. There were no other boats in the water.

"Yet the boat turned over. All on board were drowned. Sarah Fear, her brother, her niece and nephew, and a servant."

"Whew!" Chip let out his breath, shaking his head.

Corky stared at Sarah Beth, listening to her story in rapt silence. *So that explains the four graves around Sarah Fear's grave,* she thought. *A brother, a niece, a nephew, and a servant.*

"They all drowned," Sarah Beth said again, speaking softly, leaning over the table. "All within view of the shore. Maybe a five- or ten-minute swim at most."

Sarah Beth sipped her tea, then licked her pale lips. "No one knows why the boat turned over, no one knows why everyone drowned. It's all a mystery."

Corky stared down at her mug of hot chocolate, thinking hard, Sarah Beth's scratchy voice still echoing in her ears.

It was the evil spirit, Corky thought. *It had to be the evil spirit that was responsible for that accident.*

She was tempted to tell Sarah Beth about the evil force, but it was late. Her hand ached, and she suddenly felt tired. Besides, she realized she didn't really trust the young woman. She didn't know enough about her to confide in her.

"There's more," Sarah Beth said suddenly. Corky saw Sarah Beth staring at her as if trying to read her thoughts. "After Sarah Fear's death, there were all kinds of stories—stories about how she and the servant who drowned had been lovers. Stories about how Sarah and the servant were seen walking in Shadyside, walking in the woods behind her house, even walking in town—long after their death.

"You know," Sarah Beth scoffed, "the usual ghost-story mumbo jumbo that the Fear family is known for."

Her attitude surprised Corky. "You don't believe it?" Corky demanded.

Sarah Beth chuckled. A smile formed slowly on her lips. "I think it's all kind of funny," she replied, locking her dark eyes on Corky's, as if trying to gauge her reaction.

Funny? Corky thought. Five people drown? Their boat capsizes on a calm lake for no reason? Such a horrible, tragic story. And Sarah Beth thinks it's kind of funny?

Corky took a final sip of her hot chocolate. "It's pretty late. My mom is probably worried. I didn't tell her I'd be gone this long." She gave Chip a push to get him moving.

"Nice meeting you," Chip said to Sarah Beth. He slid out of the booth and reached for Corky's wind-breaker, hanging on a hook on the back wall.

"I enjoyed talking with you," Sarah Beth said, her eyes on Corky. "I usually don't meet such nice people in a cemetery."

"Are you leaving too?" Corky asked, standing up and allowing Chip to help her put her coat on.

"I think I'll stay and have another cup of tea," she replied. "I live so close. I haven't far to walk."

They all said good night again, and Chip and Corky made their way down the narrow aisle, past the counter where the two white-haired men still sat hunched over their coffee mugs, and out the front door.

"She's nice," Chip said, glancing up at the moon, which was now pale white and high in the black sky.

53

"I guess," Corky replied without enthusiasm. "But there's something odd about her, don't you think?"

"Odd?" Chip shook his head. "Just her voice."

Corky stared through the restaurant window and focused on the back booth. She could see Sarah Beth Plummer sitting alone against the back wall, her slender hands wrapped around a white mug of tea.

To Corky's surprise, she had the strangest smile on her face.

Not a pleasant smile, Corky realized.

A cruel smile.

Even from that distance, even through the hazy glass, Corky could see the gleam in Sarah Beth's dark eyes, the unmistakable gleam of . . . evil.

Chapter 7

Cheers and Screams

After school on Monday Corky hesitated at the double doors to the gym. On the other side she could hear shouts and the thunder of sneakers pounding over the wooden floorboards. The basketball team must also be practicing in the gym, she realized.

Taking a deep breath, she closed her eyes, said a silent prayer, and pushed open the swinging doors. As if on cue, the voices of the cheerleaders rang out:

> *"Hey, you!*
> *Yeah, you!*
> *Are you ready?*
> *Our team is tough and our team is steady!*
> *We're on the way to the top*
> *And we'll never stop!*

The tigers are on the hunt.
Hear them growl, hear them roar!
You'd better hold your ears,
'Cause the Tigers will roar
All over,
All over you!"

The cheer ended with an enthusiastic shout, and each of the five girls performed a flying split, their legs shooting out as they leapt into the air one at a time.

"Pretty good. Pretty good," Miss Green, the advisor called out with her usual restraint, hands on the hips of her gray sweats, her expression thoughtful. A compact woman with frizzy brown hair and a somewhat plain face, Miss Green had a husky voice that always sounded as if she had laryngitis.

"Try it again," she told them, "and this time get more height on those jumps. And *enunciate*. I want to hear consonants, guys! We're not entering the Mumbling Olympics."

On the other side of the gym, Coach Swenson was blowing his whistle. The shrill sound echoed off the tile walls. Corky watched the basketball players form a line to practice running lay-ups.

She turned her attention back to the cheerleaders, who were in position to do the cheer again. As Corky's eyes moved from girl to girl, a flood of memories washed over her, holding her in place, frozen against the doors.

There was Kimmy, the captain, her round face pink as usual, her black crimped hair bobbing on her head as she enthusiastically jumped into place and checked to make sure the other girls were lining up correctly.

Beside her stood freckle-faced, redheaded Ronnie, looking like a kid in gray sweat shorts and a white sleeveless T-shirt, whispering something to Debra.

Debra smiled slowly, her cold blue eyes lighting up. Beside her, Megan Carman and Heather Diehl, best friends who always seemed to be together, were chatting animatedly.

Kimmy blew a whistle and the cheer began.

Corky watched them run through it again. It was crisper this time, and the flying splits were higher. Ronnie started hers too soon and landed awkwardly, but everyone else was right on the money.

As the cheer ended, Kimmy noticed Corky. She jogged over. "Hi! You came!"

"Yeah. I'm here," Corky said, smiling. "The routine looks excellent!" She took a few steps away from the door.

A basketball bounced toward them. Kimmy caught it on the bounce and tossed it back to Gary Brandt, who was waving for it across the floor.

"Good to see you, Corky. We've missed you," Miss Green said, joining Kimmy. She turned back to the others. "Hey, look who's here!"

"Are you coming back?" Heather asked, as the girls surrounded Corky. They all began asking her questions at once.

"Give her a break!" Kimmy cried, laughing. She whispered to Corky, "Hey, it's like you're a superstar or something."

"With Corky back, we can do the diamond-head pyramid," Megan said excitedly. "You know, the way

57

you and Bobbi showed us." She blushed, instantly regretting mentioning Bobbi's name.

"We can try," Corky said quickly, seeing how uncomfortable Megan was. She smiled at her. "But it's going to take me a while to get in shape." She patted her stomach. "Pure flab. I feel as heavy as a bag of potatoes."

"You look *great!*" Kimmy gushed. The others quickly agreed.

Did Miss Green coach them to encourage me? Corky suddenly wondered. Or are they really happy to have me back?

Only Debra seemed unenthusiastic. As Corky went over to the wall to toss down her backpack, she saw that Debra was following her.

"I can feel it," Debra said quietly.

"Huh?" Corky propped the backpack against the wall near the other ones lined up there and turned to face Debra.

"I can feel it right now," Debra whispered, her intense blue eyes staring into Corky's. She nervously fingered the crystal she wore around her neck.

"Feel what?" Corky asked edgily. She felt nervous enough coming back to the squad. She didn't really need Debra acting so mysterious, did she?

"The evil spirit," Debra whispered, glancing at the other cheerleaders, who had begun practicing round-offs.

"Debra—" Corky started.

"I'm not trying to scare you," she said sharply. "But I'm into these things, Corky. I know the evil is here. In this gym. I can feel it." She clasped the crystal so tightly, her hand turned white.

Corky turned her eyes to the other girls. "Let's

discuss this later," she said. "I really need to talk to you about it. But not now."

"Okay." Debra looked hurt. "I just thought you'd want to know."

Kimmy blew her whistle. Corky saw Miss Green standing in front of her glassed-in office in the corner of the gym. She was watching them, a curious expression on her face.

"Corky, come on!" Kimmy called enthusiastically. She turned to the others, pushing her hair away from her eyes. "We'll work on round-offs in a little bit. Let's run through that same cheer so Corky can try it. You know it, don't you, Corky?"

Corky shook her head. "Not really. I just saw you do it twice. I could try to pick it up as we do it."

"Good," Kimmy said, flashing her a warm smile. "It's pretty simple, actually. Try it." She motioned for Corky to get in line.

Corky could feel her heart flutter as she took her place at the end of the line, next to Heather. "Here goes nothing," she said aloud to herself.

Heather gave her an encouraging pat on the shoulder. "Just watch me," she said, smiling. "Then you'll be *sure* to mess up!"

She and Corky burst out laughing.

Everyone's being so nice to me, Corky thought happily. But then her smile quickly faded.

Everyone's being so nice. It's hard to believe that the evil spirit may be hiding inside one of these girls.

"Okay. Ready?" Kimmy stepped forward to inspect the line, then moved back in place. "On three. One. Two. *Three.*"

"Hey, you!" the cheer began, followed by two loud, sharp claps.

"Yeah, you!" Stomp, stomp.

Corky shouted out the words, watching Heather to get the rhythm.

I think I can get into this, she thought.

And then the screaming began.

A girl shrieking in horror, so loud, so frightening. So *close,* as if she were right inside Corky's head.

The cheerleaders' voices faded as the hideous noise drowned out everything.

Corky covered her ears with her hands, but the shrieking continued.

"Help her! Somebody help that girl!" Corky cried, closing her eyes tight, trying to shut out the terrifying screams.

Opening her eyes, she saw that the girls had stopped cheering and were all staring at her in open-mouthed confusion.

Chapter 8

Corky Is Captured

"Corky, what's *wrong?*" Kimmy rushed over to her.

As soon as the cheering stopped, the screaming stopped too. Corky blinked hard, her heart pounding. She felt dizzy. Even though the shrieks had quieted, the sound echoed in her mind, refusing to fade.

Kimmy gently gripped Corky's shoulders. "What happened? Are you okay?"

Corky's eyes moved from one startled face to another. "Didn't you hear the screaming?" Corky asked.

Heather and Megan shook their heads and glanced at each other. Debra stared hard at Corky. Ronnie lowered her eyes. Miss Green had disappeared into her office before the cheer began.

"We didn't hear anything," Kimmy said softly. "Do you want to go sit down?"

"No." Corky shook her head and forced a smile. "Guess I'm hearing things."

"Really. Sit down. Get yourself together," Kimmy urged, gesturing toward the sidelines.

"No. Let's start again," Corky insisted.

Debra was fingering her crystal, squeezing it in her fist. When she saw Corky looking at her, she tucked it back under her T-shirt.

"Really," Corky insisted, stepping back into the line. "I want to try it again."

Reluctantly Kimmy moved back to the other end of the line. Ronnie asked her a question. Kimmy shrugged. The other girls moved into place.

I'm *going* to do this, Corky told herself. I'm *going* to succeed.

She arched her back, straightened her legs, and waited for Kimmy's count.

I'm *going* to do it this time.

But as soon as the girls started cheering, the frightening screams returned.

Again. Again. A terrified girl in some kind of terrible trouble. High-pitched, shrill—screaming for her life. Inside Corky's head.

"No! Please, please!" Corky cried, covering her ears, dropping to her knees.

The cheer stopped. So did the screams.

Kimmy reached down, took Corky's hand, and gently helped her to her feet. "Corky, what *is* it?"

"The screams. I heard them again," Corky managed to stammer, her voice breaking.

The gym spun in front of her. At the other end of the floor, some of the basketball players had stopped practicing and were asking what the problem was.

It was all a blur to Corky now. A blur of colors and hushed voices.

Kimmy led her gently to the wall. "Do you have a headache?" she asked.

"No," Corky said uncertainly. "I don't think so. I mean—I just heard someone screaming." She stared at Kimmy. "You really didn't hear it?"

Kimmy shook her head. "I'll go get Miss Green. Maybe we should call a doctor or something."

"No!" Corky said sharply. "I mean—no doctor. I'll be okay. I'll just sit down and watch for a bit. Then maybe I'll do some round-offs with everyone. You know—limber up."

What am I saying? she asked herself, the brightly lit gym still spinning in front of her. I'm babbling like an idiot.

What is *happening* to me?

Her face taut with worry, Kimmy spread out her coat for Corky to sit on. "You want some water or something?" Kimmy asked.

Corky could see the other girls huddled together, talking excitedly. They'd steal quick glances at Corky, then look away, shaking their heads.

They all think I'm crazy, she thought glumly.

"Corky, can you hear me?" Kimmy asked, standing over her.

"Oh. Uh . . . sorry. No, thanks. I don't need water." She stared up at Kimmy, forcing a smile. "I'll be okay. Go ahead—do the cheer. I'll watch."

Kimmy turned and started to jog back to the others.

What is that strange smile on Debra's face? Corky wondered. Debra was once again fingering the crystal on her neck. Her smile was smug.

Why does she look so pleased? Corky asked herself.

Debra caught Corky staring at her, and whirled away.

Kimmy shouted for the girls to line up. "Everyone ready?"

Seated on Kimmy's coat, Corky pressed her back against the tiles of the gym wall. She shut her eyes and took a deep breath.

"Hey, you!" The girls began the cheer.

The hideous screams returned.

So loud. So close.

Corky leapt to her feet, trying to locate the screaming girl.

No one there.

The cheerleaders continued their cheer. But the terrified shrieks drowned out their voices.

"No!" Corky shrieked. "No!" Covering her ears, she ran to the door.

The screams followed her as she pushed open both doors and burst out of the gym—into the arms of the young man with the strange gray eyes who had chased her in the Fear Street cemetery.

Chapter 9

"Don't You Know Who I Am?"

With a loud gasp, Corky stared up into his startled face.

His eyes really were gray. Like those of a ghost. Like monster eyes.

He gripped her arms tightly above the elbow.

He was wearing a brown leather bomber jacket. The leather felt cool against her arms. His breath smelled of peppermint.

"Let go!" Corky cried, regaining her voice.

His strange eyes narrowed. His expression changed from surprise to menace.

"Let go!" She pulled back out of his grasp.

"Hey!" he cried angrily.

She spun around and started to run, her sneakers thudding hard on the concrete floor.

"Stop!" he shouted, his voice reedy, high-pitched.

Who *is* he? Corky wondered. Why is he following me? How did he *find* me?

She glanced back and saw that he was chasing her, his expression angry, his arms out as if preparing to grab her.

She ran wildly past a blur of lockers and up the stairs at the end of the corridor.

"Stop!" he called, close behind her. His boots pounded thunderously over the floor.

At the top of the stairs Corky gasped in a mouthful of air, turned to the right, changed her mind, took the corridor to her left, running as fast as she could.

"Help me! Somebody!" she called breathlessly.

But the hall was deserted. The wall clock read four twenty-five.

"Somebody—*please!*"

She glanced back to see him emerge at the top of the stairs. He looked to the right, then spotted her in the hallway to the left.

"Wait!" he called and began running toward her, his expression hard, angry.

She uttered a low cry and turned the corner, searching frantically for a hiding place.

An idea flashed into her mind—she could duck into an open locker and pull the door shut. But the lockers on both sides of the hall were all locked.

"Hey!" She could hear him calling to her. He was about to turn the corner.

A sharp pain stabbed her side. She sucked in a mouthful of air, her mouth dry, her forehead throbbing.

I can't keep running, she thought, hearing his

footsteps near the corner. She hurled herself through an open classroom door to her right and pressed her back against the wall.

Had he seen her? Would he burst in after her?

Seeing the long tables, the tall stools, the Bunsen burners and other equipment, Corky realized she had ducked into the science lab. She wanted to call to Mr. Adams—sometimes he stayed late, grading papers in the small office at the back.

But she could hear the footsteps of the young man right outside the lab door. She couldn't call out. She could only hold her breath and pray, her back pressed against the wall, her side still aching with pain, her forehead still throbbing.

Would he run past the door—and keep on running?

Would he give up and leave?

She listened hard.

His footsteps stopped. "Hey!" he called.

He was just outside the lab door.

Corky shut her eyes and silently repeated, "Don't come in, don't come in, don't come in . . ."

She heard him hesitate.

She heard him kick a locker door.

Would he notice the open lab door? Would he look inside? Would he see her standing there, hiding from him?

If he came in, she'd have no way out, Corky realized.

She'd be trapped. Trapped like one of the mice Mr. Adams kept in the cages on the windowsill.

"Don't come in, don't come in, don't come in . . ."

And then she heard him begin to run again. She heard his heavy boots heading on down the hall.

Corky moved away from the wall, allowing the breath she had held so long to escape her body in a loud sigh.

He's leaving.

He's heading down the hall.

I fooled him.

Leaning against a lab table, lowering her head, she took a slow, deep breath. Then another.

She raised her head and listened.

Silence.

She waited.

Silence.

She waited to hear him return. But the hall remained silent. "I'm okay," she said aloud. "I'm okay." Except that her knees trembled and her head still throbbed.

She took a reluctant step toward the door—and a bell went off in the hallway right outside the door. Like a metallic siren, it clanged out four-thirty.

Corky jumped, startled. She backed into a lab table with a hard jolt. "Ow!"

When the bell finally stopped, the silence seemed deep and heavy.

"I needed that," she said sarcastically. "Stupid bell."

Her heart still pounding, she made her way to the lab door, then stepped cautiously out into the silent hallway.

A hand grabbed her shoulder roughly from behind.

The young man spun her around. His almost blank eyes burned into hers.

"Let *go* of me!" Corky cried in a tight, high voice she didn't recognize.

68

"We have to talk," he said. "Don't you know who I am?"

Corky shook her head. "No. Who are you?"

His eyes narrowed. He tightened his grip on her shoulder.

"I'm the evil spirit," he told her.

Chapter 10

"I'm Your Evil Spirit"

"Huh?" Corky's mouth dropped open. She could feel her knees start to buckle.

He was gripping her with both hands now, staring into her eyes, studying her face—studying her *fear*.

"I'm the evil spirit," he repeated, smiling for the first time.

"No," Corky whispered. "Let me go. Please."

To her surprise, he let her go. She toppled backward into the wall. She rubbed her arms, uttering a soft cry.

"You really looked scared," he said, the lower half of his face covered in shadow. His eyes continued to stare at her like two car headlights coming out of the darkness. "I think you really believed me for a moment."

"Why—" Corky waited for her heart to stop thudding. "Why did you say that? Who are you, really?"

She pressed her back against the wall, her eyes darting down the hall as she thought about an escape route.

"You ran away from me as if I *were* the evil spirit," he said. "You were scared of me. You were terrified, weren't you? And you had good reason to be!"

"Who are you?" Corky repeated impatiently.

"I'm Jon Daly," he told her. "Jennifer's brother."

Corky uttered a cry of surprise. "Her brother? I didn't know she had a brother."

"Now you do, and now you know why I followed you," Jon said, enjoying her shock.

"No," Corky told him, her voice trembling. "No, I don't. Why did you follow me? Why did you chase me?"

"Because I don't believe all the garbage I heard," Jon said bitterly.

"Garbage? What garbage?" Corky cried, genuinely confused.

"All the garbage about how my sister was invaded by an evil spirit. I don't believe in evil spirits."

"I do," Corky said softly. "I was there that night in the cemetery. I had to fight with Jennifer, with the evil that was inside her."

"Sure, *you* want to believe it," Jon said angrily. He balled his fists at his sides as if preparing to attack her. "You want to believe you killed an evil spirit *because you don't want to admit that you killed Jennifer!*"

"Now, wait—" Corky started. She could feel the fear returning, feel her knees go weak, her temples start to pound. "Wait a minute, Jon. I'm not a murderer. Your sister—"

"You killed her," Jon said, inches from her, leaning into her. "You killed my sister. Then you made up that ridiculous story. My sister wasn't evil, and she didn't deserve to die. *You* are evil—and I'm going to prove it."

"No. Your s-sister—" Corky stammered in protest. "The spirit—"

He gripped both of her shoulders. "I told you," he said angrily, "I don't believe in spirits. But you know what, Corky? I'm going to be *your* evil spirit."

"Huh? What do you mean?"

"I'm going to watch you. I'm going to follow you—you and your friends—until I find out the *truth*. Until I can *prove* that you killed my sister!"

"What's going on?" a voice called urgently from down the hall. Corky turned to see a large figure jogging toward them.

Jon released her shoulders and spun around to face the intruder.

"Corky, are you okay?" It was Chip.

"Chip!" Corky called gratefully.

As Chip approached, Jon turned away from Corky and started off in the other direction. As Chip caught up to her, Jon disappeared around a corner.

Corky sank back against a locker, trying to catch her breath.

"Who *was* that? Are you okay?" Chip asked, his eyes focusing down the hall, watching to see if Jon returned.

Corky nodded. "Yeah. I'm okay, I guess."

"But who *was* that?" Chip demanded. "What did he want?"

Corky took a deep breath. She held on to Chip's broad shoulder. He felt so solid, so safe. "He's Jennifer's brother," she told him. "Jon Daly. He's the one who's been following me."

Chip slapped his forehead with an open palm. "Jon Daly. Of course. How could I forget him?"

Corky leaned against Chip as she asked him to walk her to her locker. She'd forgotten to take her jacket to the gym earlier. "What do you mean?" Corky asked. "You know him?"

Chip shook his head. "No. But I remember him. He's the guy who went ballistic at Jennifer's funeral. Remember—they practically had to hold him down?"

"It's all a blur," Corky admitted. She tugged at her locker door.

"He's a strange guy," Chip said, shaking his head, glancing back down the hall. "He's messed up, I think. He was always in trouble. He even got kicked out of school."

"Huh? He did?" Corky asked, holding Chip's hand tightly.

"Yeah. Four or five years ago when he was a senior. I don't remember the whole story. He got into some kind of trouble—beat up a teacher, I think. Got suspended from Shadyside. Then his parents sent him away, to a military school."

"Wow." Corky let out a long breath. Her hand trembled as she worked the combination to open her locker. "He thinks I killed Jennifer."

"Did he threaten you?" Chip asked, hovering over her as she picked up her jacket, which had fallen to the locker floor.

"Kind of. He said he's going to watch me," she answered. "He said he's going to watch all of us— until he finds out the truth."

"Lots of luck," Chip said dryly.

"He's really messed up about his sister. He doesn't

believe what happened. But—but—I lost a sister too," Corky said bitterly, slamming her locker door shut. "That's what I *should* have said to him."

Chip put a comforting hand on her shoulder. "We'll have to watch out for him," he said quietly. "He seems like a bad dude."

They made their way back downstairs, where Chip picked up Corky's backpack. Then they went out of the building, into a blustery gray afternoon. "He's a bad dude," Chip repeated.

How bad? Corky wondered. Bad enough to do her harm?

Chapter 11

Two on a Grave

After dinner that night Corky went upstairs to Sean's room, to play a Nintendo basketball game with him. The phone rang and interrupted them. "Don't answer it," Sean ordered, his eyes on the screen, his fingers furiously pressing the controller.

"I have to answer it," Corky said, setting her controller down and hurrying across the room. "We're the only ones home, remember?"

"Well, I'm not going to pause it. I'm going to keep playing," Sean threatened. "You're going to lose."

Corky hurried across the hall to her room and picked up the phone on her night table. It was Kimmy.

"Oh, hi," Corky said unenthusiastically. The Nintendo game had managed to push the frightening events of the afternoon from her mind. Hearing Kimmy's voice brought them all flooding back to her.

"I just wondered how you're feeling," Kimmy said.

"Okay. I guess," Corky answered. "I mean, I can't really explain—"

"No need," Kimmy said quickly.

"I really wanted to come back on the squad," Corky said, nervously twisting the phone cord around her wrist. "But the screams—"

"Don't give up," Kimmy told her.

"I don't know. I—"

"Don't give up," Kimmy repeated. "You can do it, Corky—I know you can. Come to practice tomorrow."

Corky unwound the cord from her wrist, then twisted it around again. "I don't know. I don't think so."

"Give it another try," Kimmy urged. "Come after school tomorrow."

"I—I can't," Corky said, letting go of the phone cord and pressing her hand flat against the green and yellow patterned wallpaper. "I just remembered. I have to take a makeup exam tomorrow. In the science lab."

"Then come on Friday. That's our next practice," Kimmy insisted. "Don't give up, Corky. Try one more time. We really want you back."

Corky felt her throat tighten with emotion. Kimmy was going out of her way to be nice to her. "Thanks, Kimmy," she managed to utter. "Maybe I'll come. I really don't know what to do. I just want things to be normal again. But every time I try, something happens and—" She just had to blurt it out. "It's the evil, Kimmy. The evil spirit. It's back. It didn't disappear that night."

"What? Corky, listen—" Kimmy sounded very concerned.

"No. Listen to me," Corky insisted, more shrilly than she had intended. "What do you think caused those awful, frightening screams in my head? The evil spirit did. It was *there*, Kimmy. It was right there in the gym with us!"

"Corky, what are you doing now?" Kimmy asked softly, calmly.

"Nothing. Just playing with Sean . . . putting off doing my homework. Trying not to think about anything," Corky told her.

"Want to come over here? We could talk. You could tell me what you've found out about the evil. We could try to make a plan," Kimmy suggested.

"Well . . ." Corky couldn't decide.

"You don't want to be alone in this," Kimmy said. "If the evil is back, all of us are in danger, Corky. We're all in this. We're *all* involved. We have to work together to find it before anyone else gets hurt."

"Well, I have to stay with Sean till my parents get back," Corky replied. "But, yeah, sure. I'll be over in half an hour or so."

"Okay," Kimmy said. "We can talk then. We can talk all night if you want. I'll even help you study for that science test you have to make up."

"Thanks, Kimmy," Corky said with genuine gratitude. She hung up, feeling a little cheered.

"The game's over. You lost," Sean announced as she returned to his room.

"It's okay. I would've lost anyway," she told him, thinking about Kimmy. "Want to play another game till Mom and Dad get home?"

He shook his head. "No, I'm going to play against the machine. It's more fun."

"Oh, thanks a bunch!" Corky cried sarcastically. Then she heard the front door slam downstairs. Her parents were back.

A few minutes later she was in the car, her science text and binder on the seat beside her. She backed the car down the driveway and headed toward Kimmy's house.

It was a cold, clear night. An enormous orange moon hung low in the charcoal sky.

It doesn't look real, Corky thought. It looks like a moon in a science-fiction movie. Everything seemed sharper and brighter than it should have been. As she made her way down Fear Street, Corky felt as if she could see every blade of grass, every leaf, in sharper-than-life focus.

She followed the curve of the road, and the Fear Street cemetery came into view on her left. Her headlights swept over it, bringing a row of jagged tombstones into focus.

"Oh!" Corky cried out when she saw someone moving among the graves.

She slowed the car, her eyes on the moving figure. The orange balloon of a moon floated low over the scene. Corky stared hard, startled by the clarity. There were no shadows.

Who is it? she wondered. Who is there?

And then she recognized her.

Sarah Beth Plummer.

Without realizing it, Corky had stopped the car in the center of Fear Street. Puzzled, she rolled down her window to see even more clearly.

Sarah Beth was huddled low, moving slowly between the pale gravestones. She was wearing a long black cape that swirled behind her shoulders even though there was no wind.

What is she doing? Corky asked herself. Sarah Beth had told Chip and Corky that she had finished her work in the cemetery.

So why was she there among the old graves tonight?

Her eyes on the dark caped figure, Corky lifted her foot from the brake, and the car began to glide slowly forward. As it moved, Corky realized that Sarah Beth wasn't alone.

Another dark figure stood very close beside her, one hand resting on a tall gravestone.

With a gasp of surprise, Corky stopped the car again. In the surprisingly bright light from the low-hanging moon, it was easy to recognize the other figure.

Jon Daly.

Jon Daly and Sarah Beth Plummer. Together. In the Fear Street cemetery.

"What's going on here?" Corky asked in a whisper, her eyes locked on the two figures, so sharp and clear despite the darkness of the night.

Sarah Beth gestured with her hands. Jon stood as still as the gravestone he leaned against. Then Sarah Beth pointed to the ground.

What were they saying? What were they doing?

Staring hard, Corky recognized the stone Jon was leaning against. It was Sarah Fear's grave marker.

As Corky continued to watch, Sarah Beth suddenly pulled off her black cape and draped it over a marble monument. Then she began to twirl, raising her arms above her head, performing a slow, graceful dance.

As Sarah Beth danced, Jon still leaned against the

gravestone, not speaking, his strange, nearly colorless eyes staring at Sarah Beth.

What is going on? Corky wondered.

With a shudder of fear, she removed her foot from the brake, slammed it down hard on the gas pedal, and roared away.

PART TWO

Here Is the Evil!

Chapter 12

Surprise in the Science Lab

"We'll have to do this on the honor system," Mr. Adams said, winking at Corky as he handed her the exam.

Seated on a tall metal stool, Corky leaned forward over the lab table and took the exam from the teacher. "What do you mean?" she asked, studying his face.

Mr. Adams was young, in his mid-twenties, but his dark brown hair was already graying at the sides, and his mustache, which rested over his top lip like one of the bushy caterpillars they had studied in biology, was also sprinkled with gray. He had friendly brown eyes, a nice smile, and usually dressed in jeans and oversize sweaters. He was a tough teacher, demanding, but well liked.

"I have to go pick up my car at the service garage," he told her. "I should be back in twenty minutes, half an hour at the most." He lifted his down jacket off a chair.

Corky glanced quickly at the test. Six essay questions. No real surprises. "I'll try not to cheat *too* much while you're gone," she joked.

Mr. Adams chuckled. He pulled the bulky jacket on over his sweater. "Those frogs are noisy, aren't they?" he asked, pointing to the big frog case on the shelf against the wall. Six or eight frogs were croaking throatily. "Whoever told them they could sing?"

"They'll keep me company," Corky replied, watching the creatures hopping around behind the glass. "How long do I have for the exam?"

"It shouldn't take more than an hour," he said. "It's way too easy."

"Yeah, right," she said, laughing.

He gave her a quick wave, pointed to the paper as if to say, "Get to work," and hurried out of the lab.

The room grew silent except for the rhythmic croaking of the frogs. Corky turned her eyes to the windows that ran along the wall to her right. Shards of December sunlight slanted into the room through the venetian blinds, falling onto the large tropical fish tank in the corner. Beside it stood a human skeleton, hunched on its stand, its shoulders slumped forward, its knees bent, as if it were weary.

Shelves beside the skeleton held large specimen jars filled with insects, plant specimens, and all kinds of animal parts. Corky made a disgusted face, remembering the cow eyeball Mr. Adams had shown them earlier that afternoon. It was so enormous, so *blobby*.

She glanced up at the clock. A little past three-thirty. Cheerleading practice would be starting in the gym. She tapped her pencil rapidly on the tabletop, thinking about her long conversation with Kimmy the night before.

Then, scolding herself for wasting time, she lowered her eyes to the exam and read the first question. "Good," she said out loud, seeing that it was about osmosis. She had studied osmosis well; she knew everything there was to know about it.

She scooted the stool closer to the counter. Then she wrote the number 1 at the top of the page.

"Hey!" she cried out, startled, as the door to the room slammed shut.

Had Mr. Adams returned already? She spun around to see.

No one there.

Someone out in the corridor must have closed it.

She glanced up at the clock. Three thirty-five.

"I'm wasting time," she said and began to write.

The singing of the frogs seemed to grow louder. Glancing up with a sigh, Corky saw that the frogs were all hopping around wildly in their glass case, splashing each other, grappling onto one another's backs.

"Thanks for the help, guys," she said dryly, rolling her eyes. "What's your problem, anyway?"

She returned her attention to the test paper.

Then the venetian blinds all slammed shut at once. The clatter made Corky drop her pencil. It fell to the floor and rolled under the table.

"Hey!"

The room was much darker without the sunlight.

Corky slid off the stool and dropped to her knees to retrieve her pencil.

When she stood up, the overhead lights flickered off.

"What?"

Corky blinked. Total darkness now.

The frogs sang louder. Corky covered her ears with her hands.

"What's going on? Is someone here?"

The singing of the frogs was the only reply.

She stood, uncertain, leaning against the tall lab table. Her eyes adjusted slowly to the dim light. "Is there a blackout?" she wondered out loud.

Then she heard an unfamiliar *pop-pop-pop*. It took her a while to realize it was the sound of the glass lids popping off the specimen jars.

She saw the lids fly up to the ceiling, then crash back to the floor, the glass shattering, flying across the floor.

The contents of the jars floated up. Hundreds of dead flies rose up from one jar and darkened the air. Dozens of caterpillars followed them, floating silently in formation like a flock of birds.

The croaking became deafening.

As she stared in disbelief, Corky realized that the frogs were free. Their glass case had also shattered. About two dozen of them were leaping over the countertops, scrabbling toward her.

"Help!" Corky managed to yell.

She gasped as something large and soft plopped onto the counter in front of her, splashed her, spread stickily over her test paper.

The cow eyeball.

It stared up at her as if watching her!

The frogs were on her countertop too, leaping over one another, climbing onto the disgusting eyeball, crying out their excitement.

The venetian blinds began to clatter noisily, open-shut, open-shut, flying out into the room as if blown by the wind even though all the windows were closed.

Sunlight flashed on and off, as fast as Corky could blink.

I have to get out of here, she told herself.

She brushed a croaking frog off her shoulder. Another one leapt at her face. The cow eyeball rose up, plopped down again, then rose up as if trying to fly.

With a disgusted cry, Corky ducked as the wet eyeball flew at her face. It floated over her head. She could feel it spray her hair. Then she heard it land with a sickening plop on the floor.

She had started running to the door when something at the front of the room caught her eye. The skeleton. It was no longer hunched over. It was standing straight, straining to free itself from its pedestal.

Corky grabbed the doorknob and pulled. The door wouldn't budge.

"Help!"

She gasped as the room filled with a foul odor that invaded her nostrils, choked her throat. So sour.

Sour as death.

She tried the door again. "Help me! Is anyone out there?"

Silence.

"Please! Help me!"

And then over the clatter of the flying venetian blinds and the mad croaking of the frogs, she heard a disgusting crack. So dry. The sound of cracking bones. And, looking to the front of the room, Corky saw one bony hand break off the skeleton.

She watched, frozen in horror, as the hand, its fingers coiling and uncoiling as if limbering up, floated up over the countertops.

The now handless skeleton continued to strain against its stand, attempting to free itself.

The bony hand flew toward Corky as if shot from a gun.

Corky tried to cry out, tried to duck. But the hand zoomed in on her, flew over the wildly hopping frogs, over the quivering eyeball, through the curtain of dead insects that choked the air.

The hand slammed into her, grabbed her by the throat. The force of the collision sent her sprawling against the door.

"Help me! Somebody!" she shrieked in a voice she no longer recognized.

And then the fingers tightened around her throat. The cold, bony hand squeezed tighter, tighter.

Tighter. Until she could no longer breathe.

Chapter 13

Cut

Corky noisily tried to suck in a deep breath. But the bony fingers dug farther into her throat, tightening their already steely grip. The room pulsed with noise. The clanking of the fluttering blinds competed with the frantic croaking of the frogs. The light brightened again, then dimmed.

Then stayed dim as the hand choked off the last of Corky's air.

She whirled around and tried to slam the hand against the wall. Then she reached up with both hands and grabbed the hand at the wrist. It felt so cold. Cold and damp, as if it had just risen from a wet grave.

The room spun. The dark ceiling appeared to lower on her.

Corky grabbed the wrist with both hands and tugged. The bony fingers dug deeper into her throat, squeezing tighter.

91

She reached for the fingers. Grabbed two in each hand.

And pulled with all her might.

The sickening sound of bones cracking gave Corky some hope. Suddenly she could breathe. She noisily sucked in air, exhaled, sucked in more.

The broken fingers grasped frantically for her, but their hold was weak. She grabbed the cold wrist, pulled the broken hand off, and heaved it across the room.

Then, with a cry of horror, of disbelief, of relief all mixed in one, Corky lurched for the doorknob again and frantically turned it. This time the door opened.

She found herself in the dark, silent corridor.

She slammed the lab door hard behind her.

Her heart pounded. The only sound now.

Her eyes were clouded by tears.

She pushed her hair back from her face and started to run.

"Chip," she said out loud. "Chip!"

He had told her he'd be working late in the woodshop. They had made plans to meet there after her exam. "Chip!"

Off-balance, the floor tilting ahead of her, Corky started to run down the long hallway, her footsteps echoing loudly. She was breathing noisily through her open mouth. "Chip!"

She rubbed her throbbing throat as she ran. The bony fingers were gone, but she could still feel them pressing against it, so cold and wet, until she couldn't breathe.

"Chip!"

The shop was downstairs at the back of the building. She stumbled on the first step but thrust out both hands and caught herself on the railing.

Isn't anyone here? she wondered. The vast school building was so silent that she imagined she could hear her thoughts echoing in the hall.

Down the stairs and along a shorter hallway. The double doors to the shop came into view. The silence gave way to a high-pitched roar. A steady whine.

What *is* that noise? Corky wondered.

She pushed her way through the double doors, bumping them open with her body, and lunged into the shop.

"Chip! Where are you?" she cried, her voice revealing her terror. "Chip?"

The steady roar grew louder, closer.

Her eyes darted over the worktables, the pile of lumber against the side wall, the tall power drills, the safety goggles hanging on their pegs.

"Chip, where *are* you? Are you here?"

She made her way into the center of the big room, her sneakers sliding over the fragrant sawdust on the floor. She came to a halt at the dark puddle.

What is that?

She stared down at it. It took her a long time to realize she was staring at a puddle of blood.

Then she saw two shoes on the floor. Legs. Almost hidden behind a worktable.

Taking a deep breath, she made her way around the dark puddle to get a better view. She cried out when she saw Chip lying facedown in a larger puddle of blood. A lake of dark blood.

"Ohh."

She grabbed the top of the worktable, leaned against it, forced herself not to drop down beside him.

"Chip?"

She could tell that he was dead.

Chip was dead. Sprawled there in his own blood.

She had to look away. She couldn't keep on staring at him.

She glanced up—and saw the power saw. And realized the steady whirring sound came from the power saw. The blade was spinning loudly.

Louder.

Even louder.

And then Corky's ear-piercing screams drowned out the roar of the whirring saw blade as she caught sight of Chip's severed hand. Chip's hand, cut off at the wrist, rested like a glove beside the blade.

Chapter 14

Where Is the Evil Spirit?

Corky didn't cry at Chip's funeral.

She was all cried out. She had cried until her eyes burned and her cheeks were red and swollen. And then, suddenly, her tears were gone, as if she'd used up her lifetime's supply. She was hollow now, drained of all emotion.

Except for the sadness.

The sadness remained. And behind it lurked the terror. The frightening memories. The terrifying scenes that she knew would remain forever in her mind.

The thoughts followed her everywhere she went, kept her wide awake at night. Something was wrong in the world. Something was there. In her life. Something evil, something inhuman. Something out of control.

After the funeral she walked by herself from the

small chapel, out into a gray, blustery day. A circle of swirling brown leaves danced over her shoes as she stepped onto the sidewalk.

Dead leaves.

Death. Everywhere.

Corky turned up the collar of her coat, more to hide her face than to protect herself from the gusting winds. She jammed her frozen hands deep into her coat pockets and started to walk.

"Hey, Corky!" Kimmy came jogging up to her, her black crimped hair bobbing, her cheeks bright red, her dark eyes watery and red rimmed. Without saying a word, Kimmy threw her arms around Corky's shoulders and hugged her, pressing her warm cheek against Corky's cold face.

After a few seconds Kimmy stepped back awkwardly, shaking her head. "It's so awful," she whispered. She squeezed the arm of Corky's coat. "And you found him. You were the one who—" Her voice caught in her throat. "I'm so sorry, Corky."

Corky lowered her eyes to the pavement. More brown leaves scrabbled over her shoes, tossed by the wind.

Ronnie and Heather appeared, their faces pale, their expressions grim. Kimmy hugged them both. They offered low-voiced greetings to Corky. Then the three girls headed off toward Kimmy's blue Camry, parked across the street.

"Call me," Kimmy called to Corky. "Okay?" She didn't wait for a reply.

Corky watched them climb into Kimmy's car. She saw all three of them talking at once inside the car. As they talked, they kept stealing glances at Corky.

Corky turned away and started to walk. She had

gone several steps before she realized she wasn't alone.

"Hi, Corky," Debra said.

Her cold blue eyes peered out at Corky from under the hood of the black cape she had taken to wearing. Debra always was pale and fragile, but today she appeared almost ghostlike.

"Come talk to me," she said, her voice barely rising over the rush of the wind.

Corky shook her head. "I really don't feel like talking." She started to walk again.

Debra hurried to keep up with her. The wind blew back her hood, revealing her short blond hair. "We have to talk, Corky. We *have* to," she insisted.

"But, Debra—"

"Over there." Debra grabbed Corky's arm and pointed toward a small diner across the street. "Just for a few minutes. We'll grab a hamburger or something to drink. I'll buy. Okay?"

Debra was pleading so hard that Corky felt she had no choice. "Okay," she said, sighing. "Actually I haven't eaten today."

A pleased smile crossed Debra's face as she grabbed Corky's arm and pulled her across the street.

A few minutes later they were seated in a tiny booth, their coats folded beside them. Debra was eating a bacon cheeseburger and french fries. Corky, realizing she wasn't as hungry as she thought, took a few spoonfuls from a bowl of vegetable soup.

"People say such dumb things at funerals," Debra said, wiping ketchup off her chin with a napkin. "I heard someone tell Chip's mom that it was a really good funeral." She shook her head. "Now what's *that* supposed to mean?"

Corky stared down at the soup. "I don't know. I think people feel so uncomfortable at funerals, they don't know what they're saying," she told Debra. "People said some pretty weird things to me at Bobbi's funeral."

Bobbi's funeral.

Chip's funeral.

There had been so many funerals in her life recently.

She forced down a few more spoonfuls of soup. It didn't taste great, but the warm liquid was soothing on her throat.

"We have to talk about the evil spirit," Debra said suddenly, lowering her voice even though they were the only customers in the diner.

Corky sighed. "Yeah. I know." She stirred her soup, but knew she couldn't eat any more.

"You and I both know that the evil spirit killed Chip," Debra said heatedly. "He didn't accidentally cut off his hand and stand there bleeding to death without calling for help or anything."

"The doctors said he probably sawed off his hand and then went into shock," Corky said.

"Do you believe that?" Debra demanded.

Corky hesitated, then shook her head. "No."

"For one thing, Chip was a careful guy. He wouldn't stand there and slice off his entire hand."

"I know," Corky said, her voice catching in her throat.

"Also, do you know how hard it would be to slice your hand clean off? If you just nicked your wrist, you'd pull it away immediately. You wouldn't keep right on sawing!" she exclaimed.

"Debra, please." Corky turned her eyes to the front of the diner. Through the window she could see that wet flakes of snow had started to fall.

"The evil is still alive, Corky," Debra continued. "I know it, Kimmy knows it, and you know it. We can't just ignore it. We can't pretend it isn't there and hope it'll go away and everything will be nice again."

"I know, I know," Corky wailed. "I know better than anyone, Debra."

Debra reached across the tabletop and squeezed Corky's hand. "Sorry. I just meant—"

"The evil revealed itself to me," Corky told her. "Just before Chip—just before I found Chip."

Debra lowered her cheeseburger to the plate. She stared at Corky as if trying to read her mind. "What do you mean?"

Corky took a deep breath and told her everything that had happened in the science lab, starting with the door slamming shut and the lights going out, ending with her desperate struggle with the skeleton's hand.

Debra listened in silence, resting her chin in her hands. Both girls ignored their food while Corky told her frightening story.

"I don't believe it," Debra said softly. "I don't believe it."

"There's more," Corky said softly, raising her eyes to the window in front. The snow was turning to a bleak wet drizzle.

"Go on," Debra urged. "Please."

Corky told her about her encounters with Jon Daly and Sarah Beth Plummer. Then she told about driving past the Fear Street cemetery, about seeing Sarah Beth and Jon in the cemetery together.

"What were they doing?" Debra asked, removing her chin from her hands and sitting up straight.

"I don't know," Corky told her. "It was so strange. I saw Sarah Beth perform a dance on Sarah Fear's grave."

"You mean while Jon was watching?" Debra asked.

"Jon leaned on the gravestone and watched," Corky said. "It was so creepy."

"The evil spirit is definitely alive," Debra said in a whisper.

"But where?" Corky asked. "Why didn't it stay down in the grave? Where is it?"

"I think I know how to find it," Debra said mysteriously.

Chapter 15

Razzmatazz

> *"We've got razzmatazz!*
> *Pep, punch—and pizzazz!*
> *Hey, you—you've been had.*
> *Shadyside Tigers got razzmatazz!*
> *RAZZMATAZZ!"*

As they repeated *razzmatazz*, the five cheerleaders performed flying splits. Then they landed on their feet and, with a whooping cheer, ran to the sidelines clapping.

"Wow! That was *awesome!*" Corky cried, pushing up the sleeves of her Tigers sweatshirt as she moved toward them.

"How about the flying splits?" Kimmy asked, her expression concerned. "High enough? I had the feeling Megan and I were a little late."

"Looked excellent to me," Corky told her, grinning. "Don't be so hard on yourselves."

"Yeah!" Ronnie piped up. "If Corky says it was awesome, it was awesome!"

Everyone laughed.

Kimmy has really improved, Corky thought happily. She's much more graceful. She's even lost some weight.

It was nearly four weeks after Chip's funeral, and Kimmy had persuaded Corky to come to cheerleading practice once again. "We all have to stick together," Kimmy had urged Corky. "If we're going to find the evil, if we're going to fight it, we have to work together. If you're not on the squad, you're not really with us. You're alone."

Kimmy's words had touched Corky, had convinced her. Now here she was, ready to give it another try.

The girls, dressed in tights, denim cutoffs, and oversize T-shirts, seemed relaxed and enthusiastic, and glad to see Corky again.

"You ready to try the routine now?" Kimmy asked Corky.

Corky didn't hesitate. "Yeah. I'm ready." This time she wasn't going to be stopped.

She knew that next Saturday night was one of the last basketball games of the season. If she was going to get back on the squad, it was now or never.

Corky glanced across the brightly lit gym. Standing against the wall outside her office, Miss Green flashed her a thumbs-up sign.

Corky returned the signal and stepped into line next to Kimmy. "You have to help me with the handclaps," she said. "I think I'm straight on everything else."

"I never get them right either," Kimmy joked, giving Corky an encouraging smile.

Waiting for Kimmy to begin the cheer, Corky felt a moment of panic. The bright gym seemed to fade behind a curtain of white light. Silence seemed to encircle her.

I'm all alone, she thought. All by myself out here.

But then the cheer began, the white light dimmed, and the rest of the world returned.

> *"We've got razzmatazz!*
> *Pep, punch—and pizzazz!*
> *Hey, you—you've been had.*
> *Shadyside Tigers got RAZZMATAZZ!"*

Shouting at the top of her lungs, Corky moved easily through the routine. And when it came to the finale of flying splits, she timed her jump perfectly and leapt higher and cleaner than any of the other girls.

The routine ended with a whooping cheer, and the girls jogged to the sidelines clapping. Corky took a deep breath—and realized she was laughing, laughing from sheer joy, from the happiness of being able to perform an entire routine.

Before she realized what was happening, she was surrounded by the others. They were laughing too, eager to congratulate her, to compliment her on her performance, to welcome her back.

"Now that you're back, we can do the diamond-head pyramid again," Kimmy exclaimed. "You know, the one you and your sister invented."

"Yeah, let's try it," Corky said with enthusiasm.

"Now?" Kimmy asked, expressing her surprise.

"Yeah, right now," Corky insisted, smiling. "If we're going to do the pyramid Saturday night at the game, we'd better start now."

"You'll have to run us through it," Kimmy said uncertainly.

Corky saw Debra and Ronnie whispering intensely near the wall. "No problem," Corky said, signaling everyone to follow her to the center of the floor. "Bobbi and I spent so much time on this routine, I think I could do it in my sleep."

"Who's going to take the top?" Ronnie asked, stretching her legs.

"I will," Corky told her.

She saw the doubt form on Kimmy's face. "Corky," Kimmy whispered confidentially, leaning close, "are you sure? Don't you want to take it easy?"

"No." Corky shook her head emphatically and stepped back from Kimmy. "Either I'm going to be back on the squad just like before, or I'm not," she insisted.

Kimmy quickly relented.

"Maybe we should warm up a bit first," Debra suggested. "You know. Do some roll-ups into partner pyramids before we try the big pyramid?" She cast Corky a pleading look.

"We're already warmed up," Corky replied.

"Corky's right," Kimmy told Debra. "Let's just do it, guys."

Corky quickly outlined the pyramid to them. Three girls—Kimmy, Debra, and Heather—formed the bottom tier. Two girls—Megan and Ronnie—would stand on their shoulders, then move into liberties, each girl raising her outside foot and holding it up as

104

Corky mounted to the top to stand on Megan's and Ronnie's shoulders.

They all worked on shoulder mounts and dismounts for a few minutes; then Corky guided them into position for the pyramid.

I wish Bobbi were here, she found herself thinking. She was the real expert at getting this going.

But then she pushed Bobbi from her mind, shaking her head hard as if shaking her thoughts away. "Ready?" she called. "Let's try it now. Take it slowly. Don't worry about the timing."

"Heather, bend your knees," Kimmy instructed as Megan and Ronnie performed their shoulder mounts to form the middle tier.

Before she realized it, it was Corky's turn to move.

Before she realized it, she was climbing into position. Off the floor. Climbing so high.

And even with all of her concentration, the thoughts came rushing back. The fears. The memories.

The questions.

Will I start to hear the screaming girl again?

Will I freeze up at the top?

Will the room start to spin or go crazy?

Megan and Ronnie each grabbed one of Corky's hands and tugged. Corky stepped off Kimmy's shoulders and climbed.

Higher.

Uh-oh, she thought. Now is when the trouble comes.

Uh-oh. Uh-oh. She held her breath. Her temples throbbed.

She could feel the panic well up. Could feel it deaden her legs—could feel the fear rise up from her

105

stomach, tighten her throat. She could feel it pulse at her temples, hear it ring in her ears.

Uh-oh. Now is when the trouble comes. Now. Now. *Now.*

She stiffened her knees and raised her hands high. Balance. Balance. She concentrated with all of her will.

Uh-oh. Now. Now!

And there she was—on top of the pyramid!

Shaky. But there.

No voices. No spinning walls. No shrieks of terror. No evil.

"Congratulations!" Corky heard a voice call from the floor. "Excellent!"

She peered down to see Miss Green applauding, a broad smile on her usually dour face. "Now, watch the dismount. Take it slow, okay?"

A few seconds later the girls were on the floor, congratulating one another enthusiastically. Even Miss Green joined in the celebration.

"We did it—and no broken bones!" Corky exclaimed.

To Corky's surprise, Kimmy threw her arms around her and smothered her in a warm hug. "I *knew* you could do it!" Kimmy gushed. And then, in a whisper, she added in her ear, "Maybe the evil has left us— maybe the nightmare is finally over."

"Carry these for me," Debra said, handing the bundle of slender red candles to Kimmy. Debra wrapped her black cloak tighter around her neck.

The full moon rose over the trees. The wind sent dry leaves scampering over the weeds and tall grass.

Behind them on the street, a car rolled silently by, only one headlamp lighting its way.

"I can't believe you talked me into this," Kimmy said grumpily. "This is so stupid."

"We'll go back to my house afterward," Corky offered. "We can order pizza."

"Stop complaining. The weather's not so bad," Debra said, leading the way up the hill.

The dead grass clung to their boots. Somewhere in the distance the wind toppled a garbage can. The lid clattered noisily. A cat wailed, sounding human, like a baby.

The three girls stopped at the front walk, the concrete broken and crumbling. They stared up at the ruins of the old mansion.

"Wow," Corky whispered. "I've never been this close."

The stone walls of the mansion were charred black, evidence of the fire that had destroyed it decades before. All of the windows had been blown out. Only the front one was boarded up with a large sheet of plywood. The rest were gaping holes, revealing darkness behind the crumbling walls.

"Hey, look!" Kimmy bent down and picked up something from the dead grass beside the broken walk.

Corky shone the flashlight on it. It was a doll, wide-eyed and bald, one arm missing.

"It looks old," Debra said, examining it closely.

Kimmy dropped it to the ground. "What are we doing here?" she repeated. *"Look* at this dump."

"I know what I'm doing," Debra replied mysteriously. She gripped a large black-covered book in her hand, gesturing with it toward the door. "Let's go inside."

"I don't think so," Kimmy said unhappily, her eyes surveying the burned walls.

"Come on," Corky said, tugging at Kimmy's arm. "It's worth a try."

"I know what I'm doing," Debra repeated seriously. "Visiting the Simon Fear mansion makes perfect sense to me."

"None of this makes perfect sense," Kimmy grumbled, shifting the candles to her other hand. "How can going into this burnt-out old wreck on the coldest night of the year make any sense?"

"Do you want to locate the evil spirit or don't you?" Debra snapped, losing her patience for the first time.

"We do," Corky answered quickly.

"What makes you think we're going to find it here?" Kimmy demanded. She kicked the old doll away. It bounced across the walk and lay sprawled facedown in the grass.

"Sarah Fear spent a lot of time in this house," Debra explained. "If the evil spirit is hers, this is the most logical place for it to hang out."

"Logical," Kimmy muttered sarcastically.

"You're being a bad sport," Corky scolded. "This is better than studying for the history exam, isn't it?"

Debra focused on Corky, a hurt expression on her face, which was shrouded in the black hood of her cape. "You don't believe me, either? You're not taking this seriously?"

"I take the evil spirit *very* seriously," Corky told her in a low, somber voice. "I want to know where it is. That's why I agreed to come with you."

"I take it seriously too," Kimmy insisted. "But I

don't think we're going to get anywhere poking around and lighting a bunch of candles in this burned-out old mansion."

"Well, we have to do *something!*" Corky cried heatedly. "Maybe Debra's idea *is* dumb—and maybe it *isn't*. Let's face it, Kimmy—we're desperate. We've got to act. We can't just sit around and wait to see which one of us it kills next!"

Corky's speech appeared to affect Kimmy. "You're right," she said softly, and her expression turned thoughtful as she followed the other two toward the house.

"I've been reading a lot," Debra said, making her way through the tall weeds to the front door, holding the book in front of her, pressing it against her chest as if for protection. "This old book tells how to raise a spirit. This house is *the* place to raise Sarah Fear's spirit."

She tugged at the old wooden door, and it suddenly pulled open easily. A damp, sour smell invaded their nostrils.

"I can't go in there. Really," Kimmy insisted, taking a few steps back, her features twisted in disgust.

"Here, I'll give you the flashlight," Corky offered. "Trade you for the candles."

"Having the flashlight won't help," Kimmy replied, staring into the darkness behind the open front door. "Don't you know the stories about this place? This whole house is evil!"

"The spirits are alive here," Debra said, her eyes glowing in the beam of the flashlight. "I can feel them. I know we're going to succeed."

Corky followed her into the house. Kimmy, her

hand on Corky's shoulder, reluctantly entered too. "Yuck! It smells in here," she complained.

"You'll get used to it," Debra said quietly. She led them through the wide entryway that opened into a large sitting room.

Corky shone the flashlight around the room. Wallpaper curled down from the walls, streaked with black. Dark stains covered the ceiling, which bulged and drooped. The floorboards were cracked and broken. "Watch your step," Corky warned. "Look—there are holes in the floor."

The air felt heavy and wet. The smell of mildew and decay surrounded them. The rotting floorboards creaked as the girls made their way to the center of the room.

"This is great!" Debra exclaimed, taking a deep sniff of the sour air, her eyes glowing with excitement. "I can feel the evil spirit. I really can."

"I can *smell* it," Kimmy said sarcastically.

"Hand me the candles," Debra said. She placed the book on the floor and took the candles from Kimmy.

"Shine the light down on the book, okay? I've got to find the right page," Debra instructed as she flipped through the pages.

Corky felt a cold chill run down her back. "It—it just feels so evil in here," she said, surveying the fire-stained walls, the broken floorboards.

"We each take a candle," Debra instructed. She handed Corky and Kimmy each a red one, then lighted all three.

"We kneel in the center of the room," she said, lowering her voice to a whisper.

Corky and Kimmy obediently knelt beside Debra.

"Hold the candle in your left hand," Debra instructed. "Then we put our right hands forward and clasp them in the center."

The girls followed these directions.

Suddenly the flames dipped low and nearly went out. Corky gasped and let go of Kimmy's hand.

"You felt it too?" Debra asked, excited. "You felt the spirit?"

"It was just the wind," Kimmy said, rolling her eyes. "Give us a break."

"Try to concentrate, Kimmy," Debra scolded. "We need total concentration. I can locate the spirit here. I know I can. But we have to concentrate."

"I'm concentrating," Kimmy muttered.

They held hands again. The candle flames dipped once more. This time none of the girls reacted.

"I'm going to chant now," Debra told them. "When I finish the chant, the book says we should know where the evil spirit is."

Corky swallowed hard. The rotting floorboards creaked. The candle flames dipped, then stood tall again.

This is going to work, Corky thought. The spirit of Sarah Fear *has* to be somewhere in this frightening old place.

"Give it the old razzmatazz," Kimmy told Debra.

Debra glared at Kimmy. "Ssshhh." She raised a finger to her lips and held it there. Then, closing her eyes, she wrapped both hands around her candle and began to chant.

The flickering light played over her pale, pretty face under the black hood. She chanted in a language Corky didn't recognize. At first her voice was soft, but it grew louder and stronger as she continued to chant.

Her eyes still closed, Debra began to move the

111

candle in a circle in front of her, still gripping it with both hands. Around and around, slowly, slowly, while chanting louder and louder.

Gripping the candle in her left hand and Kimmy's hand in her right, Corky stared straight ahead, concentrating on Debra's strange, musical words.

After a few minutes, Debra finished her chant.

She opened her eyes.

And all three girls cried out as the evil spirit rose from a hole in the rotting floor.

Chapter 16

He Disappeared

Corky leapt to her feet, staring straight ahead through the darkness as the creature struggled to rise into the room.

Her mouth open in horror, Kimmy grabbed the flashlight and aimed it at the hole in the floor.

The creature whimpered and scratched at the floorboards.

"It's a dog!" Corky cried.

Debra's face fell.

Corky and Kimmy rushed forward and worked to pull the dog out of the hole in the floor. "You smelly thing," Kimmy said, petting its head and scratching its ears. "How did you get stuck down there?"

The dog, a forlorn-looking mutt with damp tangles of long brown fur, licked Kimmy's nose appreciatively.

"Don't let him lick you, Kimmy," Corky teased. "You don't know where he's been."

"A dog. I don't believe it," Debra said, sighing.

Wagging its shaggy tail, the dog circled the room excitedly, sniffing furiously along the floor.

"Maybe he *smells* the evil spirit," Kimmy said sarcastically to Debra.

"Not funny," Debra muttered, gathering up the candles. "I really thought we were close to something."

"Me too," Corky said, watching the dog as it loped out of the room. "I was so scared when we heard the thing start to come up from the floorboards."

"Bow-wow," Kimmy said dryly, rolling her eyes.

"I'm not giving up," Debra insisted.

"I am," Kimmy said emphatically. "I'm freezing." She handed the flashlight back to Corky and started toward the front door.

"Kimmy, wait," Corky called. "Want to come to my house?"

Kimmy turned back and shook her head. "No, thanks. I'm going home and getting into a hot bath."

"But—"

"Let her go," Debra said glumly.

"See you in school tomorrow," Kimmy called from the front entryway, then disappeared from view.

Corky turned back to Debra, who slammed her book shut and tucked it under her arm. "I was so psyched," she told Corky. "So *psyched.*"

"Me too," Corky said.

"We're the only ones who know the evil spirit is loose," Debra said, heading to the front. "The only ones."

"Yeah, you're right," Corky agreed sadly. "My own parents change the subject every time I try to tell them the truth."

"That's why we have to do something," Debra said.

"I just keep thinking about Sarah Beth Plummer and Jon Daly," Corky said with a shudder. She pulled up the collar of her down coat and buried her face inside it like a turtle as she followed Debra to the door.

They stepped outside, surprised to find it warmer there than in the house.

"Yeah. That sounded like a pretty bizarre scene, the two of them in the cemetery," Debra said thoughtfully. Her expression brightened. "You know what? We should check them out."

"You mean go talk to them?" Corky asked, following her toward the street.

Debra nodded. "Yeah."

"Right now?" Corky asked, glancing at her watch. It was nearly ten.

"Why not?" Debra asked.

"Well . . ." Corky hesitated. That nice hot bath Kimmy had talked about sounded pretty good to her too.

"Come on. We'll take my car," Debra urged, pulling Corky by the arm. "It'll only take a few minutes to drive to Jon Daly's house."

"Yeah, but what do we say when we get there?" Corky asked. "We can't just barge in and say, 'Jon, what were you and Sarah Beth Plummer doing in the cemetery the other night?'"

"Why not?" Debra said. She pulled open the back door to her car and dumped the candles and book on the seat. "That's exactly what we'll ask." She tossed back her hood and brushed her sleek short hair with one hand. "Come on, Corky. Get in."

Corky hesitated for a long moment, then pulled open the passenger door and climbed in. Debra slid into the driver's seat and rested her hands on top of the steering wheel.

The glow of the streetlight fell over Debra's pale, slender hand.

And Corky thought of Chip.

Of Chip's hand. Lying forlornly beside the power saw.

She saw the hand, severed neatly at the wrist. And then the puddles of dark blood.

And then Chip lying facedown in his own blood.

"Corky, what's the matter?" Debra cried, seeing Corky's horror-filled expression.

Corky shut her eyes tight, erasing the picture. "Let's go see Jon Daly," Corky said, her voice a dry whisper.

The Dalys lived in the wealthy section of Shadyside known as North Hills, a few blocks from the high school. Debra pulled up the driveway to the house, a sprawling redwood ranch-style house behind a neatly trimmed front lawn.

At the end of the drive, the garage door was open. A Volvo station wagon was parked inside. Two bikes hung on the wall. Corky wondered if one of them had belonged to Jennifer.

So much death, she thought, climbing out of the car. The evil has claimed so many victims.

She and Debra walked side by side up the flagstone walk to the front door. Debra raised her finger to the doorbell, then hesitated.

116

"Go ahead," Corky urged. "We're here. We might as well talk to Jon."

Debra rang. They heard voices inside the house, then approaching footsteps.

The porch light went on. The front door was pulled open. Mrs. Daly's head appeared in a rectangle of yellow light, her expression quickly turning to surprise. "Why, hello, girls."

Her faded blond hair was wrapped in a red bandanna. Her features seemed to melt together in the harsh light.

"Hi, Mrs. Daly," Corky said, clearing her throat. "Remember me? I'm Bobbi's sister?"

"Of course," Mrs. Daly replied, eyeing Debra.

"We came to see Jon," Corky said.

Mrs. Daly's mouth dropped open.

"Who is it?" Mr. Daly's voice floated out from the living room.

"Do you have news about Jon?" Mrs. Daly asked Corky, ignoring her husband's question.

"Huh?" Corky couldn't hide her confusion. "News?"

"Who is it?" Mr. Daly said again as he appeared behind his wife. He was tall and balding. He had on a Chicago Cubs T-shirt and straight-leg corduroys. His forehead was furrowed.

The house smelled of stale cigarette smoke.

"They have news about Jon," Mrs. Daly told her husband. She gripped his hand.

"No," Corky corrected. "We came to *see* Jon."

"We need to talk to him," Debra added, self-consciously adjusting her cape.

"Oh." Mrs. Daly's face fell. The light faded from her eyes.

117

"Jon isn't here," Mr. Daly said sternly.

"We're worried sick about him," Mrs. Daly added, gripping her husband's hand. "It's been two days. Two days. We called the police."

"Huh? The police?" Corky glanced at Debra, who looked as startled as she did.

Mr. Daly nodded sadly. "Yes. Jon disappeared two days ago. We don't know *what* happened to him."

Chapter 17

Fear

After dinner the next night, Corky waited for Debra at Alma's, the small coffee shop where she and Chip had talked to Sarah Beth Plummer. The restaurant was bustling now, the booths and long counter filled with college students, laughing and talking, their voices competing with the clatter of silverware and china and the saxophones of a salsa band pouring out from the jukebox.

Debra came hurrying in, ten minutes late, her cheeks flushed from the cold. She was wearing several layers of sweaters over blue corduroys. Her eyes swept over the crowded restaurant until she located Corky in the next-to-last booth.

After making her way past a white-uniformed waitress holding a tray of glasses over her head, Debra slid into the booth across from Corky and sighed. "Sorry I'm late."

"No problem," Corky told her, her hands encircling a white mug of hot chocolate. "Where's Kimmy?"

"She's sick," Debra announced. "Her mom says she has a temperature and everything. That's why she wasn't in school today."

Corky's mouth dropped open in surprise. "Sick? Will she be okay for the game tomorrow night?"

Debra shrugged. "I hope so."

The waitress appeared, pad in hand, and stared down impatiently at Debra. "You need a menu?"

Debra shook her head. "Just a Coke, please."

"Sarah Beth Plummer lives right across the street," Corky said after the waitress left. "She pointed out the house to Chip and me that night—we sat over there." She indicated the rear booth. "And she told us about Sarah Fear."

Debra glanced at the booth Corky had pointed to. It was now occupied by four girls having hamburgers and french fries. "You think this Sarah Beth will be helpful?"

Corky sipped her hot chocolate. She made a face. It tasted powdery. It hadn't been stirred enough. "I just had the feeling that night that Sarah Beth knew a lot more than she was telling us. There was something suspicious about her, you know. Something *devious.*"

Debra's Coke arrived. She picked up the straw and blew the paper covering at Corky. "This Sarah Beth Plummer. Is she old?"

Corky shook her head. She brushed a strand of blond hair from her eyes. "No. She's young—early twenties, I think."

"What makes you think she'll talk to us?" Debra asked.

"I don't know," Corky replied. "But I think we have to try to talk to her. I mean, I saw her dancing over Sarah Fear's grave with Jon Daly. And now Jon has disappeared."

"Do you think Sarah Beth knows where the evil spirit is?" Debra asked, sipping the Coke.

"I intend to ask her," Corky replied and sighed. "This is a crazy conversation, isn't it? If anyone overheard us, they'd think we were *nuts.*"

"But we're not nuts," Debra said quickly, gesturing with both hands, accidentally bumping her glass and spilling a small puddle of Coke onto the tabletop. "The evil is real. We know that."

"I know," Corky agreed quietly.

"Let's go see what Sarah Beth Plummer knows," Debra said.

Both girls slid out of the booth and, after paying, hurried out of the restaurant.

There was no name over the doorbell, but Corky remembered the house. It was a narrow two-story semidetached redbrick structure, part of a row of small houses, most of them occupied by students from the nearby community college.

The two girls hesitated on the small concrete front stoop, staring at the curtained window beside the door. Corky raised her finger to the doorbell, then lowered it.

"What's the matter?" Debra asked in a loud whisper.

A car rolled by quickly, its headlights sending a wash of white light over them, fixing them in a bright spot.

"I just keep picturing Sarah Beth dancing in the cemetery," Corky replied. "With Jon leaning over Sarah Fear's grave." She gripped the sleeve of Debra's sweater. "She could be dangerous, Debra. I mean— *she* could be possessed by the evil." Corky shuddered. "We could be walking in to our death."

"We have to find out," Debra said in a tense whisper. "We've got to know the truth." Taking a deep breath, she reached forward and pressed the doorbell, leaving her finger on it for a long time.

They could hear the buzzer inside the house. A light went on. They heard soft footsteps; then the door was pulled open.

Sarah Beth Plummer poked her head out. She had a bath towel wrapped around her hair. She must have just washed it, Corky realized.

Sarah Beth's eyes fell on Debra first. Then she recognized Corky. "Oh, hi." Her expression was a mixture of surprise and confusion.

"Hi. Remember me?" Corky asked meekly.

"Yes. You're . . . Corky," Sarah Beth said after some hesitation.

"This is my friend, Debra Kern," Corky said.

"Come in, come in," Sarah Beth said, shivering. "It's freezing out, and I just shampooed my hair."

The two girls followed her into a small living room filled with antique furniture. Corky carefully closed the front door behind her. The room was hot and smelled of oranges. Two old oversize armchairs and a large plum-colored couch nearly filled the space. A low coffee table in front of the couch was stacked high with books, papers, and files. The walls were lined with crowded bookshelves that reached nearly to the ceiling.

Sarah Beth rewrapped the towel on her head, staring at the two girls. She was wearing an oversize man's white shirt over black leggings and woolly white tube socks.

"Can we talk with you?" Corky asked awkwardly. "I mean, is this a bad time or anything?"

"No. I guess not," Sarah Beth replied, her expression still confused. "I was just making some coffee. Would you care for some?"

"No, thanks," Debra answered quickly.

"Take off your coat," Sarah Beth told Corky. "You can just toss it over there." She pointed to one of the armchairs.

"I thought . . . well . . . maybe you could tell us more about Sarah Fear," Corky stammered, obediently tossing her coat onto the back of one of the big chairs.

Sarah Beth's mouth formed an *O* of surprise.

"If it isn't too much trouble," Corky added.

"Sarah Fear?" Sarah Beth said, eyeing both girls thoughtfully. "Well . . ."

"It would really mean a lot to us," Debra said. "Anything you know about her."

"Okay," Sarah Beth reluctantly agreed. "I mean, I don't know that much. But sit down." She gestured to the couch. "I'll just go turn off the stove. Then we can talk. I'll tell you what little I know."

"Thanks a lot," Corky replied gratefully. "I know we're barging in—"

"No problem," Sarah Beth said, waving to them to sit. She hurried to the kitchen.

"She has such an old lady's voice," Debra whispered.

"Yeah. I know," Corky whispered back. "She

123

looked surprised to see us—but not *that* surprised," she added, her eyes on the doorway to the kitchen.

"She didn't even ask us *why* we want to know about Sarah Fear," Debra whispered.

Debra edged past the armchairs and sat down on the edge of couch, sinking into the plush cushion.

Corky tried to make her way to the other side of the couch. But she accidentally bumped the coffee table with her leg, sending a tall stack of files toppling to the carpet.

"Nice move, ace," Debra joked. She tried to get up to help Corky pick up the files, but the low, soft cushion made it difficult for her to stand.

Corky dropped to her knees and began hurriedly to pile the manila files back on the table. A bunch of envelopes fell out of one of the folders.

She scooped them up and started to replace them— and then stopped. Her eyes widened in surprise.

"Debra, look!" she gasped.

"What is it?" Debra asked.

"These envelopes . . ." Corky said, her voice trembling. "They're all addressed to Sarah *Fear!*"

Chapter 18

Sunk

"Sarah *Fear?*" Debra grabbed an envelope from Corky's hand and pulled it close to study it. "But this letter was postmarked only a few weeks ago!" she exclaimed.

Corky glanced nervously to the doorway. "Do you think Sarah Beth Plummer is really Sarah Fear?" she whispered, frantically stuffing the envelopes back into the folder.

"You mean—is she over a hundred?" Debra asked.

"The furniture is all so old," Corky remarked. "Sarah Fear would feel comfortable in this room."

"I'm back." Sarah Beth reappeared, carrying a cup of steaming coffee. She stopped just past the doorway. "Corky, what are you doing down there?"

"Uh . . . I accidentally knocked some stuff over," Corky confessed, staring hard at Sarah Beth.

"Oh, don't worry about it," Sarah Beth said, moving toward one of the armchairs. "This place is a mess. I'll pick it all up later."

"Uh . . . Sarah Beth?" Corky started. She held up one of the envelopes. "I couldn't help but see. These letters—they're all addressed to Sarah Fear."

Sarah Beth's eyes narrowed for a brief second, but she quickly resumed her friendly expression. "I know," she told Corky.

"But—"

Sarah Beth lowered herself carefully into the big armchair, sinking deep into the cushion, resting the coffee cup on the padded arm. She sighed. "Well, I guess you know my secret. I'm a Fear."

Corky gasped.

Sarah Beth laughed. "It isn't *that* terrible! It doesn't mean I'm some kind of demon, you know!" She seemed to find Corky's reaction very amusing.

Corky climbed to her feet and joined Debra on the couch. "So your real name is Sarah Fear?" she asked, staring into Sarah Beth's eyes as if trying to read her mind.

Sarah Beth nodded. "I don't use it. Most of the time I use my mother's maiden name—Plummer." She took a sip of coffee. "The Fear name is such a curse."

"What do you mean?" Corky asked, clasping her hands tightly in her lap.

"Your reaction said it best," Sarah Beth replied, smiling. "When I said I was a Fear, you practically fainted on the floor!"

All three of them laughed.

"I was just . . . surprised," Corky explained.

"Surprised and horrified," Sarah Beth added. "Everyone in Shadyside knows that the Fear family is

126

filled with weirdos and monsters. The name *is* a curse." All the amusement drained from her face. She took a long sip of coffee. "A *curse.*"

"Are you related to the first Sarah Fear?" Debra asked. "Are you named after her?"

"I'm related to her somehow," Sarah Beth replied. "I don't know if my parents named me after her or not—I don't think so." She reached up with her free hand and pulled the towel off her head. Her black hair, still wet, fell down around her face. She tossed the towel over the chair.

"I've spent my whole life trying to get away from that dreadful name," she said with emotion. "Fear." She made a disgusted face. "But it's funny—I find myself drawn to the story of the Fears. I'm fascinated by my ancestors, drawn to them, pulled to them as if by an invisible force."

"When we talked the last time," Corky started, "across the street, at the restaurant—"

"I didn't tell you everything," Sarah Beth interrupted. "I confess." Her dark eyes burned into Corky's. "I didn't reveal everything I know about Sarah Fear. I just didn't want to." She paused, and then her expression hardened and she added, "I really don't want to now."

Corky recoiled at the young woman's sudden coldness. She glanced at Debra, who was staring intently at Sarah Beth.

"We really need your help," Corky said, her voice cracking with emotion. "My sister and my friends—Bobbi and Chip and Jennifer—they've all lost their lives. And I don't know. Maybe I'm next."

Surprise registered on Sarah Beth's face. She set her cup down on the carpet at her feet.

"Something evil killed Bobbi and Chip," Corky continued. "Something evil from beyond this world. And we think it has something to do with Sarah Fear."

"That's why we have to find out all we can about Sarah Fear," Debra said, shifting her weight on the couch. "We need to know everything you know so that maybe we can stop this evil."

Sarah Beth stared at Debra as if seeing her for the first time. "I don't understand," she said finally. "I really don't think my dredging up ancient history will do you any good."

"Please!" Corky cried, not intending to sound so shrill, so desperate. "Please, Sarah Beth, please help us. Please tell us what you know."

Sarah Beth raised both hands as if surrendering at gunpoint. "Okay. I'll talk, I'll talk!" she cried. "Don't shoot."

"First tell us what you and Jon Daly were doing in the cemetery the other night," Corky said. The words just burst out of her. She hadn't really intended to ask that question till later.

Sarah Beth acted surprised. "You were there?" she asked Corky. "In the cemetery?"

"No. Just driving by," Corky explained.

Sarah Beth blushed. She took a deep breath. "I didn't think anyone saw us." She stared at Corky.

She's stalling, Corky thought. She's thinking fast, trying to think of a good lie. "I saw you dance," Corky said, staring back at Sarah Beth, challenging her with her eyes.

Sarah Beth chuckled and shook her head. "It was all so silly."

"Silly?" Corky asked. She was determined not to let Sarah Beth off the hook.

"I've known Jon for years," Sarah Beth said, her cheeks still pink. "We were in school together. We even dated for a while, but I lost touch with him. When he called me a few weeks ago, I was really surprised."

"He called you?" Corky asked.

Sarah Beth picked up the coffee cup and took a long sip. "Yeah. Out of the blue. He was really pumped, sounded a little crazy to me. But Jon was never exactly what you'd call calm."

"What did he want?" Debra asked, tucking her legs under her.

"He wanted me to meet him. In the Fear Street cemetery," Sarah Beth replied, reaching up and fluffing her still-damp hair. "Jon knows that I'm a Fear. And he knows about my interest in my ancestors— and my interest in spirits and the occult."

She finished her coffee and set the cup back down on the carpet. "So I met him at the cemetery," she continued. "He was definitely acting weird. I mean, really weird. Even for Jon. As soon as I got there, he started asking me if I knew the truth: the truth about his sister, Jennifer. I really didn't know what he was talking about."

Corky stared intently at Sarah Beth, listening, studying her eyes. I don't think she's telling us the truth, Corky thought. There's something wrong with this story.

"Then Jon started asking me if I believed in evil spirits. I told him I believed in all kinds of things— but that didn't seem to satisfy him. He knew I studied the occult and the spirit world. He asked me if I knew how to summon spirits from the grave. At first I just laughed at him. I thought he was kidding me."

She shook her wet hair. "Are you two okay? Do you think it's too warm in here? I could turn down the heat."

"No, we're fine," Debra replied quickly. "Please—go on."

"Well, I didn't really want to continue. But Jon was so insistent. He was really out of his head. I told him I'd read about a dance you do on someone's grave to summon the dead person's spirit. He demanded that I show it to him. I felt ridiculous, but he wouldn't take no for an answer. So I showed him a little bit of the dance. I mean, actually I made up most of it—I don't really know it." She turned to Corky. "I guess that's when you drove by."

But you seemed to be really *into* it, Corky thought skeptically. You didn't act like it was some kind of goof, Sarah Beth. You looked really serious to me.

"Then what happened?" Corky asked.

"Nothing," Sarah Beth replied with a shrug. "Nothing happened. No spirit appeared—big surprise, huh? I thought Jon would be disappointed, but he looked very pleased. Really happy, for some reason. Then we said good night and went our separate ways. I haven't seen or heard from him since."

Something's wrong here, Corky thought. There's something wrong with this story.

"What a strange guy," Sarah Beth said thoughtfully. "He's scary, I think. Really scary."

The room grew silent. A clock somewhere in the back started to chime. Corky glanced at her watch. Nine o'clock.

"Sure I can't get you some coffee?" Sarah Beth offered. "It's all made."

"No, thanks," the two girls said, again in unison.

"Then I guess I'll tell you about Sarah Fear," Sarah Beth said, stifling a yawn. "That's why you've come, right?"

"Yes. We really need to know about her," Corky said, studying Sarah Beth's face.

"I'm afraid you'll be disappointed," Sarah Beth told them. "I don't know all that much. Most of it I got from old newspapers and what few family records I could find. One of Sarah's cousins, Ben Fear, kept a journal. That was helpful up to a point. But believe me, there are a lot of gaps in the story. A lot of gaps."

She tucked her legs beneath her in the big chair, leaned on one of the overstuffed arms, and began to talk, moving her eyes from Corky to Debra, then staring down at the dark carpet as she spoke.

"I guess I'll begin with Sarah's death. Or I should say, *near*-death. That would be in . . . uh . . . 1899, I guess. Up to that point, I think you could say that Sarah had managed to escape the curse of the Fears. Meaning she had had a fairly happy life.

"In his journal, Ben Fear described her as a lovely flower of a young woman. That's the way Ben wrote. He was pretty flowery himself. But I guess it can be said that Sarah was beautiful in every way. She was a lovely young woman, kind, generous, and loving.

"I'm starting to sound like Ben Fear," Sarah Beth muttered, rolling her eyes. "Oh, well, bear with me. According to family records, Sarah was happily married. For a brief time, anyway. She never had any children.

"She and her husband lived close to Simon Fear's mansion. Their house was always filled with people. Cousins, friends, servants. It was quite a life.

"And it didn't change much, even after Sarah's

husband died of pneumonia. She mourned him for an entire year. Then she resumed her busy, people-filled life.

"Then in early 1899, the good life abruptly came to an end. Poor Sarah fell ill—deathly ill. I don't really know what the sickness was. Perhaps no one back then knew either. In his journal, Ben Fear described it as a 'wasting disease.' Old Ben had a way with words, didn't he?

"Well, the doctors gave up on Sarah. She was given up for dead. In fact, a grave was dug in preparation, in the Fear Street cemetery. And a minister was called upon and told to prepare a funeral ceremony.

"But then there was some kind of miracle. To everyone's surprise, Sarah Fear didn't die. In fact, she made a remarkably fast recovery. Her strength seemed to return overnight. And despite the pleas of her family to rest and regain her energy, she pulled herself out of bed the very next day and returned to her duties of running the house.

"Here's where the story gets strange. After her illness, Sarah changed. She wasn't the same sweet 'flower' anymore. According to Ben Fear's journal, she became withdrawn, reclusive. She developed a terrible temper and was known to throw tantrums for no apparent reason. She turned away from all of her friends.

"The details in the diary become sketchier and sketchier toward the end of her life. My theory is that Ben Fear was no longer invited to Sarah's house, and so he had little firsthand information about her to write in his journal.

"He did tell of rumors that Sarah and a servant had become lovers.

"There were reports of strange gatherings in her house. Late-night meetings. Séances. Wild parties. The police reports are very discreet. Don't forget— Simon Fear was still around, still a powerful figure in the town. Nevertheless, the scandalous stories about Sarah began to spread.

"The newspaper became full of frightening stories about the events that took place at Sarah's house. One spring day a kitchen maid was found murdered in the garden, stabbed through the heart with an enormous pair of hedge shears. A houseguest was also murdered, his leg severed, cleanly cut off his body and found lying beside him on the floor of the stable.

"Sarah Fear was never under suspicion for these murders. And the mysteries were never solved.

"Then came the biggest and most tragic mystery of them all. The pleasure boat trip. Sarah Fear's final trip. It took place on Fear Lake. You know. Tranquil, flat Fear Lake. The tiny, round lake behind the Fear Street woods.

"There were five people on the boat. Sarah Fear. Three of her relatives. And one servant. According to the newspaper report, it was a beautiful summer day, a perfect day, no clouds, no wind.

"Sarah's large pleasure boat sailed away from the shore. And a few minutes later it happened—from out of nowhere. A mysterious hurricane-force gale. Totally unexpected—on the calmest, most beautiful day of the summer. A wind so powerful that it capsized the large boat. Turned it over in a flash.

"And everyone drowned. Everyone, including Sarah Fear. Within view of shore—only a five- or ten-minute swim at most. And yet all on board Sarah's boat were drowned. There were no survivors.

133

"Which brings us to the strangest part of all," Sarah Beth said, leaning forward in her big chair, staring at the two girls across from her on the couch, lowering her voice to just above a whisper. "The strangest part of all. When the bodies were pulled ashore, their skin was bright red, blistered, and scalding hot—as if Sarah and her companions had all drowned in *boiling water!*"

Chapter 19

Did You Hear About Jon?

"Drive around," Corky said. "I don't feel like going in just yet."

"Let's park and talk," Debra said. She pulled the car halfway up Corky's driveway and cut the lights and the engine.

Corky turned her eyes to the house. The lamp over the door cast a yellow triangle of light on the front porch. All the other lights were out. Her parents were either in the back or had gone to bed early.

"Did you get the feeling that Sarah Beth was holding something back?" Debra asked, tapping her gloved hands on the steering wheel.

Corky slid down low in the passenger seat, raising her knees to the dashboard. "Yeah. I think she knows more than she let on," she agreed. "But I don't know what it would be."

"I asked her if she thought Sarah Fear had been possessed by an evil spirit," Debra said. "She just looked at me as if I were from Mars or something."

"She wouldn't answer any of my questions, either," Corky complained. "You heard me when I asked what happened to the servant who was supposed to be her lover? And all she would say was that Sarah Fear's secrets were buried with her."

Debra sighed and rubbed her glove against the side window, which was starting to steam up. "Weird lady," she said quietly.

They had left Sarah Beth's house a little after ten o'clock, their heads spinning with the bizarre details of the story she had related to them. "I hope I've been helpful," Sarah Beth had said as she walked them to the door. "If I come across anything else, I'll get in touch with you."

But Corky and Debra left with more doubts and suspicions than when they had arrived. They had driven the short distance back to Corky's house in silence, each going over in her mind what she had heard. And now they sat in Corky's driveway as the car windows steamed up around them, eager to share their thoughts.

"It's just too perfect," Debra said, squeezing the steering wheel with both hands. "She's telling us about Sarah Fear—and *her* name is Sarah Fear. It's too perfect, and too strange."

"They died in scalding hot water," Corky said thoughtfully, closing her eyes. "That's how my sister died. In the shower. In scalding hot water."

"I know," Debra said in a whisper, staring straight ahead.

"And remember the teakettle? That afternoon when I scalded my hand?" Corky cried, her mouth dropping open in horror as the memory flew back to her. "Again—scalding hot water."

"I remember," Debra said, putting a hand on Corky's trembling shoulder. "You're right. Hot water is a clue. It's definitely a clue."

"But a clue to *what?*" Corky asked shrilly, feeling her frustration build. "A clue to *what?*"

"What about those gross murders at Sarah Fear's house?" Debra asked, turning in her seat to face Corky. "The houseguest with his leg cut clean off. Just like Chip. Just like Chip's hand."

Corky swallowed hard. "I—I hadn't thought about that, Deb. But you're right."

The two girls sat silent for a long moment, staring at the steamed-up windshield.

"So what are we proving?" Debra asked finally.

"Well . . ." Corky thought hard. "I guess we're proving that it's the same evil spirit doing the same horrible things—then and now."

"And how does that help us?" Debra demanded, staring intently at Corky.

Corky shrugged. "I don't know." She shook her head unhappily. "I just don't."

"There has to be another clue in the Sarah Fear story," Debra insisted, her features tight with concentration. "There has to be a clue about how to defeat the evil spirit. Somehow the spirit ended up in Sarah Fear's grave; we know that. Somehow it was forced to stay down there for a hundred years. But how? How did Sarah Fear defeat it?"

"She didn't," Corky said dryly. "She didn't defeat it. It killed Sarah Fear—remember?"

"Oh, yeah," Debra said softly.

They lapsed into silence again.

"Now, a hundred years later, more death," Corky said, staring at the clouded windshield. "Jennifer, Bobbi, Chip . . ." A loud sob escaped her throat.

"I wonder who'll be next," Debra muttered, her eyes dark with fear.

Corky's parents were watching TV in the den in back. Pulling off her coat, she went in to say hi to them. They were engrossed in some cop show, and she could see they didn't want to chat. So Corky said good night and headed up to her room.

She didn't feel like talking to anyone. Her head felt as if it weighed a thousand pounds, weighted down by all she had heard and by her confused thoughts and theories.

If only we could trust Sarah Beth Plummer, she thought, starting to pull off her clothes and get ready for bed. But I know we can't trust her. For all we know, Sarah Beth herself could be the evil spirit!

If only we could trust *somebody*.

She pulled on a long nightshirt and deposited her clothes in a neat pile on the chair across from her bed.

Debra and Kimmy and I—we're all alone, Corky thought. We're all alone against this ancient evil force. We're the only ones who know about it. The only ones who *believe* in it. And what can the three of us do? *What?*

I don't know *what* to think, she told herself, heading to the bathroom across the hall to brush her teeth. We shouldn't have gone to Sarah Beth's. Now I'm even more confused than before.

And more frightened.

She had just started to put toothpaste on the brush when she heard her phone ringing. Dropping the toothbrush into the sink, she dashed back into her room and picked up the receiver. "Hello?"

"Hi, Corky. It's me. Kimmy."

"Kimmy!" Corky cried in surprise. "Hey, how are you feeling?"

"Better, I guess," Kimmy replied uncertainly. "My temperature is down. But I didn't call about that." She sounded breathless, excited.

"What's happening?" Corky said.

"Did you hear about Jon Daly?" Kimmy asked, nearly squeaking the words.

"What about Jon?" Corky demanded. "Did they find him?"

"Yeah, they found him all right," Kimmy replied. "They found him in Fear Lake. Drowned."

Chapter 20

A Cheerleader Falls

"How do you feel?" Kimmy asked.

"Kind of fluttery," Corky told her, swallowing hard.

Kimmy took the maroon and white pom-pom from Corky's hand and helped her untangle it. "You'll do fine," she said, flashing Corky an encouraging smile as she handed it back. "Once the game starts, you won't even think about how nervous you are."

I hope she's right, Corky thought, glancing up at the scoreboard, which was being set up for the game. The scoreboard lights were all flashing, and the clock was going haywire, the numbers running backward faster than Corky could read them.

I hope the game goes that quickly, Corky thought, fiddling with the cuffs of her white sweater. She could feel her heart racing. She took a deep breath and tried to calm herself.

A few early arrivals entered the gym and made their way to the bleachers. Corky watched them, then turned her eyes back to the scoreboard clock. About half an hour until game time.

A hand touched her shoulder. She jumped, startled.

"Sorry," Miss Green said. "I just wondered if you needed a pep talk."

Corky grinned. "Thanks. But I think I'll be okay."

"Nervous?" the advisor asked, studying Corky's face.

Corky nodded. "Yeah. But I can handle it."

"You'll be great," Miss Green said, glancing at the gym door as more people entered. "Practice has been terrific. The new pyramid routine should tear the roof off."

"If I don't fall on my face," Corky joked.

Miss Green chuckled. "You'll get your old confidence back once the game starts. You'll see." She gave Corky a thumbs-up, turned, and jogged back toward Kimmy and the other cheerleaders.

By now the bleachers were nearly half full. The scoreboard clock showed fifteen minutes till game time. The teams were warming up on opposite ends of the floor, shooting running lay-ups, several balls thundering off the basket and backboard at once.

"Show time!" Kimmy called, clapping her hands, gathering the cheerleaders together. Corky moved quickly into the circle, wiping her perspiring hands on the sides of her short skirt.

"Energy up!" Kimmy shouted. "Let's get this crowd warmed up. Let's see some *spirit!*"

The girls all cheered. Debra gave Corky an encouraging smile and a slap on the back. Forming a line, they trotted to the bleachers and began their warm-up chant:

> *"Shadyside High!*
> *Shadyside High!*
> *Can you dig it?*
> *Everybody's here.*
> *So everybody CHEER!"*

Then again. Louder. Encouraging the crowd to join in, to clap, to get loud.

And again. And again. Even louder.

And the crowd picked up the chant, picked up the enthusiasm, stomping and clapping until the nearly filled bleachers bounced and shook.

> *"Let's get a little bit rowdy!*
> *R-O-W-D-Y!"*

And again. They repeated this chant until the Shadyside fans were screaming out the word. Then they ended it with synchronized back handsprings, all six girls performing a backward flip in unison, landing perfectly before jumping up and starting the chant again.

It's going great, Corky thought with relief as the shouts and cheers echoed off the walls. I'm doing fine. I'm going to be okay.

She looked down the line of girls and saw Kimmy grinning back at her. I'm going to be okay, Corky thought.

The game started. The gym reverberated with the pounding and squeaking of ten pairs of basketball shoes and the steady thud of the ball against the shiny hardwood floor.

Corky knelt on the sidelines with the rest of the squad, watching the game, waiting for a break when the cheerleaders would go into action. She could feel her heart racing, but from excitement rather than nervousness.

The game was going quickly, a close match in which the lead kept changing sides. Corky watched intently and, when it came time to do a cheer, performed with her old enthusiasm and grace.

Standing in front of the cheering fans, the crowd stretching up nearly to the rafters, she felt as if she were shouting away her problems, roaring back at all the terrors that had plagued her.

Just before halftime she turned to see Kimmy huddled behind her. She leaned down and spoke into Corky's ear, struggling to be heard over the thunderous crowd noise. "About the pyramid," Kimmy shouted.

Corky cupped her ear and smiled up at her.

"At the end, when you're ready to dismount from the top, count to three, okay? So I can be sure I'm in position to catch you."

"Okay, gotcha." Corky nodded. "Have I been coming down too fast?"

"I just want to make sure I'm in position," Kimmy said, putting a hand on her shoulder. "So count to three, and then jump, and I'll be there."

"Thanks," Corky said. And then she added, "I'm really grateful, Kimmy. For everything."

Kimmy didn't hear her. She had moved on to give instructions to Ronnie and Heather.

It was halftime before Corky realized it. The time

did seem to be moving as fast as the scoreboard clock when it was being set before the game.

The visiting cheerleading squad performed first. They had come with a ten-piece band and did a lot of rap cheers and club-type dancing.

"They're good," Corky heard Megan say as they waited on the sidelines.

"They're *different,*" she heard Heather reply. She didn't mean it as a compliment.

A few minutes later Corky felt her excitement surge as she followed the other girls to the center of the floor to begin their performance.

The opening routines went well. Then Ronnie mistimed a backflip and landed hard. But Debra helped her up quickly, and the routine continued without a pause. There were no other mishaps.

We're doing okay, Corky thought happily. She suddenly wondered if her parents were somewhere up in the bleachers. They had talked about coming to the game and bringing Sean.

I hope you're here, Corky thought. I hope you're seeing how great everything is going. My big comeback!

And then it was time for the pyramid, the grand finale.

As the girls began their shoulder mounts, the crowd hushed expectantly.

Corky crossed her fingers for a brief second, took a deep breath, and began her climb.

Up, up.

And she was at the top. And the pyramid was formed.

Perfect.

And the crowd shouted its appreciation.

Corky smiled and thrust out her arms.

And as she focused on the top of the bleachers, the gym began to spin. The entire room began to twirl, like a carnival ride out of control.

She uttered a low cry. She felt her knees start to buckle. "What's happening?"

The walls were whirling. She was inside a spinning cyclone of light and color and noise. "No! Please!"

Struggling to keep her balance, she closed her eyes.

When she opened them, the gym was still whirling.

Faces suddenly came clear as the bleachers spun around in front of her. She saw a red-haired boy with freckles. Saw him so clearly.

The room spun around again. The whirling lights grew brighter, brighter. Swirls of red and yellow and white.

And she saw a man with a red wool scarf tossed around his neck, sitting close to the floor.

And the gym spun around again.

The shouts and cries seemed to circle her, press in on her, suffocate her as the blindingly bright gym whirled faster and faster.

And then stopped.

And she saw Sarah Beth Plummer standing just inside the double doors.

Sarah Beth Plummer?

What was *she* doing here?

I've got to get down, Corky thought, feeling cold perspiration run down her forehead, feeling her knees tremble. Got to get down.

She turned her eyes to the floor, and there was Kimmy. Ready for her. In position already—waiting. Giving her an encouraging nod.

Corky took a deep breath.

Her legs felt rubbery, weak. She leaned forward, raised her knees, tucked her legs.

And leapt.

Kimmy's face twisted into a mask of horror.

She didn't move to catch Corky. Didn't raise her arms.

And Corky hurtled to the floor, hitting hard with a sickening *thunk!*

Chapter 21

Not Okay

Corky opened her eyes to silence.

White silence.

The gym had become so quiet.

Faces emerged and came slowly into focus, blurred, distorted, shadowy faces.

"I couldn't move!" she heard a shrill voice crying somewhere above her. "I couldn't move. I couldn't raise my arms!"

It was Kimmy's voice.

The shadowy faces brightened. Corky realized she was lying on her back, staring up at the gym ceiling.

The pain was like a raging river, rolling over her entire body.

Miss Green peered down at her, her features tight with worry.

Other faces stared down.

Ronnie's face was drawn and pale. She had tear-stains on her freckled cheeks.

Debra stared down at Corky, her cold blue eyes wide, her lips pursed in fear.

She could hear Kimmy sobbing now, loud sobs.

It was so cold now. So cold and silent. And the pain was everywhere.

"I wanted to catch her," she heard Kimmy tell someone, her voice shrill and trembling. "I *tried* to catch her. But *something held my arms down!*"

That's what Bobbi had said, Corky thought.

The faces above her slipped back into darkness.

That's what happened to my sister, she realized.

Something had held Bobbi's arms down. Something had paralyzed Bobbi. Only no one would believe her.

I believe you, Bobbi. I believe you.

Because I know what was responsible. I know what did it.

It was the spirit.

The evil spirit is here.

It's right here.

But where?

It tried to kill me. It tried.

And then the most horrifying thought: maybe it *did* kill me.

The faces darkened even more.

She heard Kimmy sobbing.

And then the darkness swallowed her.

When Corky opened her eyes, a different face stared down at her.

"Mom!"

Her voice came out choked and dry.

Mrs. Corcoran, her eyes watery, smiled down at Corky. "You're going to be okay," she said, putting a cool hand on her forehead.

Corky tried to sit up, but pain forced her back onto the pillow. "Where am I?"

"You're in the hospital," her mother said. Her smile appeared frozen in place—it didn't fade, even when she talked. "The emergency room." She dabbed at the corner of one eye with a wadded-up tissue.

The room came into focus. Actually, Corky saw, it wasn't a room. Just a small rectangular cubicle with gray curtains for walls.

"You're going to be okay," Mrs. Corcoran repeated, still offering Corky that forced smile.

No, I'm not, Corky thought glumly.

"You bruised a rib. And you broke your arm. That's all," her mother informed her.

So the spirit didn't kill me, Corky thought, turning to stare at the gray curtains. It didn't kill me. This time.

But next time . . .

"Your father is filling out some forms," Mrs. Corcoran said. "When he's finished, we can go home. Isn't that great? You're going to be okay."

Corky forced a smile back at her mother. I'm *not* going to be okay, she thought. I'm *never* going to be okay.

The evil spirit had killed Bobbi.

And tonight it was in the gym. Tonight it tried to kill me.

I'm not okay. Not okay. Not okay.

A dark-haired young intern in a white coat appeared suddenly above her. "Can you sit up?" he asked, smiling. "I'd like to check the cast one more time."

Holding her by the shoulder, he helped Corky to a

151

sitting position. To her surprise, she saw a large white cast encasing her right arm.

"I wouldn't try to do any backflips for a while," the doctor joked.

"Sean, what are you doing up this late?" Mrs. Corcoran scolded.

Corky's brother, who had greeted them eagerly at the front door in his pajamas, shrugged his slender shoulders.

"He refused to go to bed," explained Mrs. Barnaby, the neighbor who had been baby-sitting. "He said he had to see his sister's cast."

"Well, back away from the door so your poor sister can get inside," Mr. Corcoran exclaimed.

Sean's eyes grew wide with excitement when he saw Corky's cast. "Wow! Can I touch it?"

Corky extended it to him. "Go ahead. If that's a thrill for you."

"No, wait," Sean said excitedly. "I want to sign my name on it. You're supposed to sign casts, right?"

"Not tonight, please!" their mother begged.

"Corky's had a rough night," Mr. Corcoran told Sean. "Give her some space."

"Can I write a message on it?" Sean asked, ignoring his parents as usual. "You know. Something funny."

"Tomorrow," Corky said shakily. "I'm really feeling kind of weird right now."

Sean made his pouty face, but backed off.

"You got two calls," Mrs. Barnaby told Corky, pulling her wool coat over her shoulders, adjusting her scarf. "I wrote them down. One from a Debra; one from Ronnie someone. I told them you were still at the hospital."

"Thanks," Corky said wearily. "I'll call them tomorrow."

Mrs. Barnaby said good night and headed for home.

Sean argued for a short while. Then he agreed to let Mr. Corcoran tuck him into bed. "Tomorrow I'm going to write something really stupid on your cast," he warned Corky.

"Thanks. Can't wait," his sister replied dryly.

"I'm going to run you a hot bath," Mrs. Corcoran told Corky. "The doctor said it would be good for your sore muscles."

Corky shrugged. "Okay, I guess."

I've been attacked by an ancient evil force, she thought scornfully, and Mom thinks a *bath* will help!

"You just have to be careful not to get the cast wet," her mother warned.

"I'll try," Corky muttered.

She followed her mother up the stairs. After entering her room, she lowered herself carefully into a sitting position on the edge of the bed.

Her ribs ached. Her arm throbbed under the cast.

I can't do anything, she thought, uttering an exasperated cry. I can't even undress myself.

She heard the rush of water in the bathtub across the hall. A few seconds later her mother appeared in the doorway, shaking water off her hand. "Let me help you change."

Corky felt embarrassed to be undressed by her mother, but she was too weary to protest. Her mother slipped a cotton robe around Corky, then helped her tie the belt. "This isn't going to be easy," she told her daughter. "But we'll manage."

Corky sighed in response and started toward the bathroom.

"Do you want me to help you get in the tub?" Mrs. Corcoran called after her. "You've got to be very careful."

"No, thanks, I'll manage," Corky said.

She stepped into the bathroom and closed the door behind her. The room was steamy and warm. The steam felt good against her cheeks.

She bent and turned off the water with her left hand.

"Just call me Lefty," she said aloud.

She stared down into the deep aqua tub. The bath looked inviting. Every muscle in her body ached.

This is going to feel good, she thought.

She had started to pull off the robe when she realized that someone was standing behind her. She turned quickly.

First she saw the maroon and white cheerleader outfit.

Then she saw the girl's face.

"Kimmy!" Corky cried in surprise. "What are *you* doing here?"

Chapter 22

Corky's Bath

The white steam rose up around Kimmy. Her dark eyes glowed in the misty light.

"I wanted to get rid of you forever," she said coldly, speaking in a low, husky voice.

Corky backed up against the closed bathroom door. "Kimmy—what? What are you saying? You're *frightening* me."

Kimmy's normally pink cheeks flushed scarlet. "I'm not Kimmy," she announced in the strange, husky voice.

"Kimmy, listen—" Corky started. Her ribs ached. Pain throbbed down her arm. "I'm so tired. I—"

"You didn't cooperate," Kimmy said, taking a step toward Corky. "You were supposed to die—like your sister."

"Now, *wait!*" Corky cried. "Kimmy—"

"I'm not Kimmy!" she snarled, then let out a roar that blew away all the steam. "I am what you fear most!"

"No!" Corky tried to shriek, raising her good hand to fend off the menacing figure before her.

The puzzle is solved, she realized, feeling paralyzed by dread, unable to move, to call for help, to take her eyes off the advancing girl.

The puzzle is solved.

The evil spirit is revealed.

It's been inside Kimmy.

"Where is Kimmy?" Corky demanded, finding her voice. "What have you done with Kimmy? Did you kill her?"

At first the creature didn't respond. Her dark eyes reddened, then glowed like fire. Her hair—Kimmy's black hair—rose up around her head, flew up like dark flames.

The low, raspy voice declared, "I have been in Kimmy ever since that night. That night in the cemetery. The night *you* thought you sent me back to my grave!"

Corky stared in silent horror into the creature's eyes, glowing like coals on a fire, at the dark hair flying wildly around its face.

"You thought you were defeating me," the evil spirit continued. "You should have known better. Ronnie was there too. And Debra was there. And Kimmy, lucky Kimmy."

"You moved from Jennifer's body to Kimmy's," Corky whispered, slumping weakly back against the door.

Kimmy's eyes grew even brighter, so bright Corky had to look away. "Why?" Corky asked. "Why are you doing this? Why did you kill Chip and Jon? Why are you trying to kill me?"

"Kimmy's enemies became *my* enemies," the voice rasped. "I paid Chip back for dumping Kimmy and for liking you. Jon was following me everywhere. He was coming too close to the truth. I knew that when I saw him with Sarah Beth." She paused. Her dark eyes narrowed icily. "He's gone now."

"But why kill *me?*" Corky cried in a shrill, frightened voice she didn't recognize.

"I have to pay you back for that night in the cemetery. You tried to destroy me. Now you must be destroyed."

"No!" Corky cried. She reached for the doorknob.

But the door wouldn't budge.

"Time for your bath," the husky voice said. "So nice of you to draw a hot, steamy tub. Now, Corky dear, you can die like your sister."

With startling strength, Kimmy grabbed Corky by the hair, jerked her toward the tub, and started to force her head down into the hot water.

Chapter 23

Down the Drain

"Ohh!" Corky tried to pull back as Kimmy pushed her head down toward the steaming tub.

But Kimmy was too powerful.

The steaming water seemed to rise up to meet Corky.

I'm going to drown, she thought.

I'm going to die now.

She closed her eyes as her face met the water.

So hot. So burning hot.

She held her breath. Twisted her body. Tried to force her head up.

Kimmy pushed with inhuman strength.

Deeper. Corky felt the water fill her ears. Rise up over her hair.

I'm drowning now.

I'm dead.

Pictures whirred wildly through her mind. Faces. All of her friends. People she didn't recognize.

Her chest ached.

I can't hold my breath much longer. My lungs are going to explode.

More pictures raced through her mind. A jumble of faces. She saw her family. She saw Sean. Sad-faced Sean.

Now he won't get to sign my cast, she thought.

He'll wake up, and I'll be dead.

Dead, dead, dead.

And Sean will be alone.

No! A voice screamed in her head.

No—*I can't let this happen!* I can't let the evil win again!

As her fear turned to anger and her anger flamed to desperate rage, Corky reared up against the powerful force with all her strength—and swung the heavy cast.

"Oh!" Kimmy groaned as the elbow of the cast clubbed the back of her head.

Momentarily stunned, her fiery eyes faded to black. She stumbled forward.

And as she stumbled, Corky stood up, water pouring off her head. She grabbed Kimmy's wildly flying black hair with her left hand, jerked the head downward with all her might—and pushed Kimmy's face into the steaming hot water.

Corky turned and, still grasping Kimmy's hair with her good hand, leaned the cast on Kimmy's head. And pushed.

Down. Down.

Kimmy's head was entirely submerged.

She struggled to get up. Her arms flailed frantically. She kicked with her legs. She strained to raise her head.

Her chest heaving, the pain shooting through her body, Corky leaned all of her weight against Kimmy's head, pushing, pushing it down, bearing down with the heavy cast.

Kimmy thrashed and fought.

She pushed up with inhuman strength, pushed up, up, strained against Corky's cast, struggling to remove her head from the water.

"Drown! Drown!" Corky said without even realizing it. "Drown! Drown!"

And then Kimmy's mouth opened wide.

A raging wind poured from her mouth.

Into the water.

A wind so hot, so fierce, the water instantly began to boil and bubble.

And still Corky pressed down. Battling the force, she pushed Kimmy's head back down, submerging it so the raging wind made boiling tidal waves roll across the tub.

The tiny room filled with steam. Thick, white clouds of it rose up from the tub, scalding hot. Corky began to choke on it.

I can't see, she realized. It's thicker than any fog.

She couldn't see her own arm. Couldn't see the cast. Could no longer see the head she was holding under the water.

The white steam grew even thicker.

Corky blindly choked, gasping for air.

And hung on.

Hung on to the struggling head as the wind raged and the bathwater tossed and churned. Hung on blindly.

I'm suffocating, she thought. I can't breathe. I'm drowning in a cloud. Drowning in a thick, scalding cloud.

Suffocating . . . like Bobbi.

But she held on. And pushed. Pushed with her remaining strength, pushed in spite of her pain, pressed the head under the rolling hot water.

The steam cleared. Corky could see again.

Under the water Kimmy uttered a loud groan.

A disgusting green liquid poured from her mouth. The stench of it rose up from the tossing water.

Corky gagged, struggled to hold her breath, trying not to breathe.

The thick green liquid oozed out of Kimmy's mouth. Took shape. Formed a long snakelike figure.

Longer, longer.

It coiled around the bottom of the tub. More. More rolled out of Kimmy's open mouth.

"Drown! Drown! Drown! Please—drown!" Corky screamed.

Leaning on Kimmy's head with the cast, she reached down and pulled open the drain.

She heard a gurgling sound.

And stared in disbelief as the foul-smelling, green liquid snake was sucked down the drain.

Chapter 24

The End?

As it oozed down the drain, the thick green liquid made a disgusting sucking sound that grew louder and louder, echoing in Corky's head, vibrating, vibrating until the walls appeared to shake.

Still holding Kimmy's head down even though the water had been drained, Corky held her breath, trying to avoid the putrid odor that invaded her nostrils.

The white steam, rising from the tub, rolled over her, wrapped her up like a hot, wet blanket.

The last of the undulating green gunk gurgled into the drain.

Corky shut her eyes. When she opened them, the steam had vanished. The room was clear.

Silence.

She stared down into the tub.

The green ooze was gone.

The water had drained out too.

Kimmy uttered a low cry.

With a sob of relief, Corky loosened her grip on Kimmy's head.

"Hey!" Kimmy cried. In her old voice, not the frightening, raspy voice of the evil spirit.

"Hey!" Bent over the empty tub, Kimmy shook her head, beads of water rolling off her black curls.

Reluctantly, Corky let go of Kimmy's head and backed away from the tub, her arm throbbing under the heavy cast, her entire body aching.

Kimmy turned around slowly, her dark eyes wide with confusion. She pushed herself up from the tub and stood breathing hard, her chest heaving. She stared at Corky as if she didn't recognize her.

"Corky?" she cried uncertainly, squinting, her mouth dropping open. Her eyes darted around the small room. "Where am I? What am I doing here?"

Despite her weariness, Corky let out a whoop of joy. "Kimmy, is it *you?*"

The question seemed to confuse Kimmy even more.

Corky offered her a hand. "Kimmy, I don't *believe* it!" She helped pull Kimmy to her feet.

Kimmy gripped the sink to steady herself. "But how . . . ? I mean, I don't understand." She suddenly reached up and grabbed her hair with both hands. "I—I'm wet. I don't—"

"Take it easy," Corky said softly. "Let's get out of here. Let's go downstairs, and—"

"But how did I get here?" Kimmy demanded. "I was in the Fear Street cemetery. You were struggling. Wrestling with Jennifer over that open grave."

"That's the last thing you remember?" Corky exclaimed. "Kimmy, that was months ago!"

"Huh?" Still gripping her hair tightly in both hands, Kimmy gaped at Corky. "Months? What do you *mean?*"

Corky started to reply, but a loud pounding on the bathroom door made her stop.

"Corky, are you okay?" her mother called in. "What's going on in there?"

Corky pulled open the door.

"Mom, it's okay."

Mrs. Corcoran gasped in shock. "Kimmy, what are *you* doing here?"

"I—I don't know," Kimmy told her, still dazed.

"Kimmy's okay," Corky told her mother. "She's okay. Let's get her downstairs."

"But she's all *wet!*" Mrs. Corcoran cried in confusion. "And so are you!"

Corky managed to calm her mother. They helped Kimmy down the stairs and onto the living-room couch. Mrs. Corcoran went into the kitchen to call Kimmy's parents to come and get her.

When her mother was out of the room, Corky moved next to Kimmy on the couch and whispered to her. "The evil. It's gone."

Kimmy started to say something, but Corky put a hand on her arm to silence her.

"Just listen to me. The evil is gone. I drowned it. Really, I drowned it. I saw it disappear this time. Maybe now the nightmare is over. Maybe it really is gone for good."

A few hours later Corky lay awake in bed, watching the shadows play across her ceiling. Her ribs ached. Her arm throbbed and itched under the cast. She shifted her weight uncomfortably.

Poor Kimmy, she thought. She was so dazed, so confused. I don't think she'll ever believe the truth.

Corky tried to turn onto her side, but a stab of pain shot across her chest. She rolled onto her back again, tugging the covers with her good hand.

Is the evil spirit really gone forever? she wondered, closing her eyes. Will my life finally return to normal?

Yes.

She answered her own question. Yes. Yes. Yes.

Happily repeating the word over and over, she fell into a fitful sleep.

The next morning she slept late. The clock radio on her night table said 11:55 when she pulled herself out of bed, yawned, and stretched her one good hand.

She stood up, feeling stronger. A little unsteady. But definitely stronger.

She looked out the window. Bright blue skies.

A sunny day, she thought, smiling.

At last! A sunny day.

The days will all be sunny from now on, she thought cheerfully. She smiled at herself in her dresser mirror.

I'm starving, she realized, pushing her hair back from her face before rubbing the sleep from her eyes.

Still in her long cotton nightshirt, she padded down to the kitchen, humming to herself. "Hey, anybody home?"

No reply.

She started to open the refrigerator, but stopped when she saw the morning mail on the kitchen counter. Shuffling through the stack of bills and mail-order catalogs, she pulled out an envelope addressed to her.

It was hand-printed in light blue ink. There was no return address.

Curious, Corky struggled to tear open the envelope

with her good hand. She pulled out a folded sheet of paper. It appeared to be a note.

"Who is it from?" she wondered aloud.

And then she gasped in horror as she unfolded it and read the brief message:

IT CAN'T BE DROWNED.

THE NIGHTMARES
NEVER END. . .
WHEN YOU VISIT

FEAR STREET®

Next . . .
CHEERLEADERS:
THE THIRD EVIL

IT CAN'T BE DROWNED! Corky Corcoran
and the Shadyside High cheerleaders know the
evil spirit is still with them. But where? And in
whom? A visit to cheerleader camp is a terrifying experience for Corky, Kimmy, Debra, and
Ronnie. Corky knows she *must* destroy the spirit
for good, before any more of her close friends
die. But this cheerleading season may be her last,
as Corky battles for her life against a spirit more
evil than anyone ever imagined!

About the Author

"Where do you get your ideas?"

That's the question that R. L. Stine is asked most often. "I don't know where my ideas come from," he says. "But I do know that I have a lot more scary stories in my mind that I can't wait to write."

So far, he has written nearly three dozen mysteries and thrillers for young people, all of them bestsellers.

Bob grew up in Columbus, Ohio. Today he lives in an apartment near Central Park in New York City with his wife, Jane, and fourteen-year-old son, Matt.